1920's Investigators' Companion Vol. II

Occupations & Skills

H. P. LOVECRAFT 1890–1937

FOR THE 1920s
INVESTIGATORS' COMPANION
VOLUME II: OCCUPATIONS & SKILLS

by

Keith Herber

with Kevin A. Ross, Gregory Rucka, and Gary O'Connell

project leader and editorial **KEITH HERBER**
graphic design and layout **LES BROOKS**
production assistance **PETRA PINO**
cover design **CHARLIE KRANK**
copyreading **SHARON HERBER**

CHAOSIUM INC.

1994

Clear Credit

THE ROLE MODEL thumbnail sketches in the Occupations of the 1920s section are by Kevin Ross. Gregory Rucka is responsible for the main body of the text of Appendix A: The Professional Investigator. Gary O'Connell for the Pro Tips interspersed throughout The Professional Investigator and most of Appendix B: 1920s Forensics. All other material by Keith Herber.

1920s INVESTIGATORS' COMPANION VOLUME II is published by Chaosium Inc.

Address questions and comments concerning this book as well as requests for free catalogs of Chaosium books, games, and supplements to Chaosium Inc. 950-A 56th Street, Oakland CA 94608-3129, U.S.A.

Chaosium Publication 2346. Published in February 1994
ISBN 1-56882-018-6

Introduction

VOLUME II OF THE 1920 Investigator's Companion contains vital information about several new skills and many new occupations appropriate for the era.

On Becoming an Investigator provides a short introduction to life as an investigator, along with a few tips to make that life a little longer and a little less unpleasant.

The Occupations section is by far the largest, containing descriptions of over 140 different possible occupations for 1920s *Call of Cthulhu* investigators. Although at first glance many may seem of little value, the listing includes many types not generally recognized by players but which nonetheless offer potential. Also, when an investigator dies or goes insane the player looking for a replacement investigator may not always be in a position to choose exactly the occupation they wish. Settling for the local bartender or streetcar conductor who witnessed the crime may be the best one can do. Additionally, keepers can draw inspired non-player characters from this list.

1920s Skills reprints the skill descriptions found in the 5th Edition *Call of Cthulhu* rulebook. Most of these skill descriptions include additional material regarding the era of the Roaring Twenties.

Appendix A tells about the professional investigator: what's legal and what's not, along with tips from an unnamed professional that give a more realistic picture of the profession.

Appendix B describes the current state of the science of forensics.

— Keith Herber

Table of Contents

PART-1

On Becoming an Investigator

Career and Finances, Friends and Family Protégés, Retirement, Libraries and Collections, Making a Will, 1920s Occupations.

IT MOST OFTEN BEGINS with a late-night phone call, or a letter from a friend in need, or a mysterious stranger who comes knocking at the door. Innocent, curious, usually looking to help someone in need, fledgling investigators begin a course of action that will leave their daily lives, careers, friends and families forever changed. Risking physical injury, death, and madness, investigators are drawn by an insatiable curiosity to explore the darker side of existence--and to learn certain secrets that mankind was never meant to know.

Career and Finances

Once entangled in these secret mysteries, an investigator's normal life begins to come apart. Among the first things to suffer is the individual's career, job, or business. Frequent, unannounced trips out of town by an employee usually result in a person being dismissed from his job. An investigator who owns his own business might leave it in the hands of a trusted partner or senior employee, but unless the investigator is totally sure of this person's character they take a risk by not attending to their own interests.

Dilettantes are in the best position. Supported by their own money, their time is their own and their finances may greatly exceed the savings of even the most penny-pinching of hard working investigators. If an investigator is not a dilettante himself, he may find it to his advantage to begin associating with one.

Otherwise, once the investigator has nearly exhausted his own savings, and perhaps converted property and real estate to cash, he may find himself in need of a loan. Banks readily lend money to new businesses--it is, after all, an age of investment and entrepreneurs. Couched in the proper terms, a bank may be interested in backing an investigator's antique shop, or chemist's laboratory.

Private investors might also be tapped. Philanthropists abound in the 1920s, many families having accumulated large fortunes are now ready to spend them on libraries, museums, scientific research, and archaeological and anthropological expeditions. Even small towns often harbor one or two rich individuals who are perhaps willing to back a small venture for the fame and credit it might bring him. Professional expertise, experience, and good Credit Rating and Persuade skills are helpful.

Short of turning to a pawnbroker, the investigator's close friends and family may be his last resort for a desperately needed loan with which to purchase information, a weapon, or a fast ticket out of town.

Friends and Family

Those close to the investigator may become distressed over this person's new, and perhaps mysterious life style. Associations with shady characters, brushes with the authorities, and stretches of time spent in jail or mental institutions often drive all but the most loyal family members away. After all, most people do not want to be associated with a 'crank.' Hence, investigators themselves, after stirring up more trouble than they've bargained for, may voluntarily disassociate themselves from friends and family, possibly fearing retaliation by some group or another that has taken offense at the investigator's actions.

But the most loyal friends and family members often stand by investigators. Unwilling to write off an old friend, favorite uncle, or close cousin, they are often instead drawn into the investigator's adventures themselves, eventually becoming steadfast associates.

Protégés

Protégés come in all shapes and sizes, and may be a favorite nephew or niece, a past student, former business associate, or even a police detective that once arrested the investigator. The important thing about a protégé is that he or she is a loyal and helpful friend.

A protégé is often first contacted when the investigator needs a certain skill or expertise that neither the investigator nor any of his present associates possess. This could be a specific mechanical skill like Pilot Airplane; an in-depth knowledge skill like Astronomy or Geology; or facility with a foreign language that allows the protégé to decipher a tome or act as an interpreter on some upcoming overseas trip. Once drawn into the mysteries already known to the investigator, protégés often become investigators themselves.

Protégés are also valuable in that they are often--at least at first--willing to take risks that the investigator is not. However, a close call or two usually instills in them a healthy respect and caution in the future. Protégés can be groomed to take over the investigator's lines of enquiry after the investigator feels he is no longer fit for active adventuring and wishes to slip into retirement.

Retirement

The costs of adventuring to an investigator's physical and mental health are enormous. Many don't live to retire, those who do are those few wise enough to know when to call it quits. Although the body heals, continued exposure to unsettling sights and the forbidden knowledge usually gained in the course of adventuring take a toll on an investigator's sanity that is often permanent. Rather than continue to risk irrevocable madness, many investigators choose to retire from active adventuring, continuing to act as consultants and researchers for other, more active investigators. Even though sometimes thousands of miles from the actual adventuring site, retired investigators can be contacted by telephone or telegraph, asked questions, or be requested to research specific topics. In truly critical situations, the experienced investigator can be brought out of retirement in order to fulfill a critical function in a current investigation.

By the time of retirement, most investigators will have acquired a certain body of knowledge, supplemented by a small library of important books, and possibly a collection of artifacts as well.

Libraries and Collections

Over the course of their careers most investigators come into possession of at least a few books of mysterious knowledge and possibly some artifacts or souvenirs from their various adventures. It may be in the best interest of newer investigators, those just graduated from protégés, to avoid reading these tomes, if possible. The retired investigator should already be familiar with the information found in a certain book, and may prove to be the most valuable researcher. Further perusals of a tome cost an investigator no additional sanity, but a fresh investigator wishing to read the book for the first time will have to pay the usual sanity costs.

Additionally, a collection of tomes and/or artifacts may someday come in handy for emergency financing. Most of these books are rare and many quite valuable. Unloading a small collection of rare tomes could support an investigator nicely for a couple years or more. Such collections also make for nice donations to museums or libraries. An investigator making out his will should give this latter option consideration.

Making a Will

Any investigator, before getting too deeply involved, should give serious thought to writing a will. Although an investigator can write his own, it is advised that a professional lawyer do the actual preparation of the document. A disputed will can be tied up in Probate Court for years, gradually sucking dry the estate while various parties contest its conditions. Professional help goes a long way toward avoiding such problems. A simple will should cost an investigator no more than $10-$20.

An investigator may wish to leave cash and property to family members, or to close friends. Where large amounts are involved, trust funds might be established, particularly in the case of minors. Investigators wishing for a little immortality might donate some of their libraries or collections to a public institution. Donors are usually credited for the donation and/or the discovery of such items.

The future needs of an investigator's protégés should, of course, also be considered. An investigator may wish to leave them with finances, libraries, and files, in order to better their own future investigations. With enough money, an investigator's will can even provide for the creation of a 'foundation' bearing the deceased investigator's name, guaranteeing him or her a certain measure of immortality.

Occupations Index

1920s Occupations

THE CHOOSING OF AN investigator's occupation is probably the most important choice a player makes. The occupation of your investigator has a direct bearing on which skills he may have, his potential earnings, his status in the community, and possible special abilities. Although the following listings may seem, at times, excessive, keep in mind that a player searching for a quick replacement character in the middle of an adventure may have limited choices. Keepers may also draw inspiration from these samples. Aside from brief descriptions of each occupation, pertinent information such as Earnings, Contacts and Connections, Skills, and sometimes Special notes are also included.

Earnings

Rather than try to indicate dollar figures, occupational earnings are given as a general level, indicative of the type of lifestyle an investigator might be able to afford. These listings are to be considered typical. Certainly any number of untypical situations can be imagined and incomes should be reduced or increased as the keeper and player see fit. Earnings can be further effected by raises, promotions, or lay-offs.

- **Pauper ($0-$250 per annum):** This income level is far below the poverty line and is typical of hoboes, indigents, and beggars. Unless the character lives at home with family, he sleeps in alleys and eats handouts or from garbage cans.
- **Lower Class: $251-$500 per annum.** This income group includes the lowest paid part-time help including migrant farm workers and part-time janitors and dish washers. Such individuals live in flop houses, YMCAs, or, at best, share cramped one-room apartments in awful neighborhoods with one or more roommates, cooking canned soups on illegal hot plates.
- **Upper Lower Class ($501-$1500 per annum):** By careful scrimping and saving this character can afford a one or two-room apartment with a kitchen, in a run-down tenement in a bad neighborhood. Bathrooms and telephones are shared.
- **Lower Middle Class ($1501-$2500 per annum):** This income level affords the character a modest one or two-bedroom apartment located in a neighborhood better than the very worst in town. The character perhaps has his own phone and, if careful how he spends his money, might be able to afford an unreliable used car.
- **Middle Class ($2500-$6000 per annum):** This level of income allows an investigator to own a modest house or rent a quality two or three-bedroom apartment. A modestly priced automobile is also within reason. You own more than one suit and can afford to treat yourself to a decent restaurant once or twice a month. A refrigerator (rather than an ice box) and other home appliances are within your reach.
- **Upper Middle Class ($6000-$25,000 per annum):** At this level of income an investigator can afford a larger house of three or four bedrooms or a expansive apartment of six or seven rooms. There is enough money to afford two automobiles of reasonable price, send your children to inexpensive private schools, have a maid in two or three times a week, and have enough money left over for a few investments.
- **Upper Class ($25,000-$75,000 per annum):** This level allows ownership of an impressive mansion with a swimming pool and tennis courts, or a penthouse apartment atop a better hotel. More than one domestic is the norm, and includes a chauffeur for the inevitable limousine. Dining out at fine restaurants and annual European vacations are the usual.
- **Wealthy ($75,000 plus per annum):** The sky's the limit: yachts, private aircraft, multiple homes, and major market investments.

Contacts and Connections

Contacts and Connections offers a general listing of different social circles, professional realms, and other areas where a character of a certain occupation might enjoy special influence or 'leverage' due to personal contacts, professional courtesy, or other. Exact details and the extent to which a character may make use of such connections is, of course, judged by the keeper.

Note that not every investigator has necessarily made all the possible connections listed and, in fact, there are some an investigator may prefer to avoid. A lawyer with numerous criminal and organized crime connections may find doubt cast upon his character. But then again, it may be that in the role of the local District Attorney his contact with local gangsters has been purely adversarial. Players and keepers will have to define such relationships if and when necessary.

Players, especially those with reporter or private detective investigators, should develop one or two specific contacts: individuals the investigator knows personally. They may be paid informants, business contacts, friends, or professional colleagues. Give these characters a name, an occupation, and define their relationship to their investigator. Although intended as the occasional helpmate, note that such characters are not necessarily wholly the creation of the player. The keeper may wish to add some background or tie to the character that the investigator has 'forgotten' about. This could be an old debt, or a favor owed, or anything else that occurs to the keeper. These contacts might occasionally become involved in adventures as protégés, perhaps even someday replacing a player's prior investigator after retirement or unfortunate mishap.

Skills

The skills listed are those considered most appropriate to the given occupation. It is from this list that skills should be chosen when spending EDU points. It is not necessary to choose *all* the skills listed, but only those that suit the investigator the player is creating.

Special

Special options are included with many of the occupations. These include bonuses or penalties to be added to abilities and skills; resistance to specific sorts of sanity loss or phobias; special skills such as Fire Fighting or Typing which, while undefined, should be self-explanatory; and others.

A few occupations, due to past events, may inflict an investigator with a small, but significant secret phobia. These may be chosen by the player himself but it is suggested that the keeper make the choice, keeping it a secret from the player until it can be revealed at a properly dramatic moment.

A number of occupations include modifiers for attributes: bonuses and penalties assigned to STR, DEX, EDU, etc. In most cases these modifiers should be applied before computing points and choosing skills. The single exception to this rule are penalties to EDU. In this single instance, points should be figured and skills purchased *before* the EDU score is reduced.

Note that all such options are exactly that, and subject to the final judgement of the keeper.

Adventurers and Daredevils

ADVENTURERS AND DAREDEVILS are part of the American scene. Aviators cross great bodies of water or frozen poles while explorers search deserts and jungles for lost civilizations. Although their skills, occupations, and conquests are widely varied, all share a love of danger and excitement.

They may become investigators after making certain chance discoveries while exploring, or when following up on the chance discovery of another adventurer, a colleague perhaps since deceased. Many of these characters may be alerted to secret mysteries when they obtain ancient maps, books, or other artifacts either on their own, or through the mail.

Big Game Hunter

Aviator

Professional aviators may be employed on U.S. contracted mail routes or work as a pilot for one of the small commercial passenger lines. Others work at carnivals, stunting or selling rides to awed rubes, or offering local 'air-taxi' service in and out of small airports. Others compete in organized air races, either cross-country or on fixed courses. Hollywood makes fair use of pilots, as do aerial mapping firms, the U.S. Forest Service, and many others. A few aviators even find work as test pilots for the aircraft manufacturers. Many actively serve in the U.S. military.

Many aviators learned to fly during the War and as a result still hold commissions as officers in the Army, Navy, Marines, or Coast Guard. Younger pilots have either received military training during peacetime or learned on their own.

American flying aces of the World War still in the public limelight include: Eddie Rickenbacker, presently employed by Chrysler Corporation; Tommy Hitchcock, Jr., now a star on the polo fields; and Reed Landis, son of Baseball Commissioner Kenesaw Mountain Landis.

There is no national regulation of pilots until the passing of the Air Commerce Act of 1926, after which time pilots' licenses are required.

EARNINGS: Upper Lower to Lower Middle class. Owning your own plane can make for sudden, unexpected expenses.

CONTACTS AND CONNECTIONS: An aviator may have old military contacts plus connections with other commercial pilots, mechanics, airfields, etc. Aircraft manufacturers might grant access to experimental designs, improved powerplants, and better navigational gear.

SKILLS: Accounting, Bargain, Credit Rating, Electrical Repair, Listen, Mechanical Repair, Navigate, Parachute, Pilot Aircraft, Spot Hidden.

SPECIAL NOTES: All aviators have an automatic beginning Air Navigation skill ("dead-reckoning") equal to half their Pilot Aircraft skill. This can of course be raised by expending additional points. They also benefit from a 20 point Spot Hidden bonus.

Race Driver

Auto racing is a favorite sport of the 1920s. The Indianapolis 500 is already a highly-publicized annual event. Many drivers race boats as well as automobiles.

EARNINGS: Widely variable.

CONTACTS AND CONNECTIONS: Away from the track the successful race driver probably has inside access to auto and boat manufacturing interests. The demand for Hollywood stunt drivers might result in connections with the film industry.

SKILLS: Drive Automobile, Electrical Repair, Mechanical Repair, Pilot Boat, Psychology, Spot Hidden.

SPECIAL: Practiced drivers and pilots can pull off certain 'stunts' with their machines, even crashing or rolling an automobile with comparative control and safety.

Charter Boat Captain

Charter boats work both coasts of America, as well as on the Great Lakes, catering to sport fisherman and vacationers. By far the greatest number of charter boats are found in Florida, on both the Gulf and ocean coasts. Those found at Key West can be chartered for trips to Havana, Cuba, where alcohol, gambling, and nearly anything else are legally available. Charter boats are typically large cabin cruisers equipped with bunks and a galley.

EARNINGS: Lower middle class or better, but an owner often lives on his boat, avoiding the high cost of rent.

CONTACTS AND CONNECTIONS: Coast Guard, smugglers, organized crime.

SKILLS: Accounting, Bargain, Credit Rating, First Aid, Listen, Natural History (Marine), Navigate, Persuade, Pilot Boat, Spot Hidden.

SPECIAL: 20 bonus points added to Spot Hidden.

Explorer

There are still enough unknown areas in the world that some people can make a career of exploring. Scientific grants, inflated by private donations combined with newspaper, magazine, book, and film rights often generate enough money to support the adventurer and his exciting life.

Still unexplored is much of darkest Africa, great portions of the Matto Grosso in South America, the great Australian desert, the Sahara and Arabian deserts, and much of the Asian interior. Although expeditions have reached both the north and south poles, much of the surrounding territory is still unknown.

EARNINGS: Middle class and higher, depending on success.

CONTACTS AND CONNECTIONS: Major libraries and universities, monied patrons, other explorers, publishers, foreign government officials.

SKILLS: Climb, Dodge, Firearms, First Aid, History, Jump, Medicine, Natural History, Navigate, Other Language, Photography, Swim, possibly Archaeology, Anthropology, or other scholarly skill.

SPECIAL: +1 to CON. Add 20 points to Persuade roll whenever dealing with a primitive people or a foreign government.

Aviator Charles Lindbergh (1902-1974)

Lindbergh is most famous as an aviator, but also dabbles in invention and, later, the anti-war movement as well. Lindbergh was born in Detroit, Michigan, but grew up in Minnesota. His father, Charles Augustus Lindbergh, Sr., was a Minnesota Congressman from 1907-1917. Charles, Jr., briefly attended the University of Wisconsin then enrolled in a flying course. In 1923 he made his first solo flight, and a year later became a cadet in the U.S. Air Service Reserve.

In 1927, while employed flying a mail route between Chicago and St. Louis, Lindbergh decided to try and win a $25,000 reward offered by a New York businessman for the first person to fly nonstop across the Atlantic. Before attempting the feat, however, Lindbergh first sets a coast-to-coast record of 21 hours and 20 minutes, with only a brief stop in St. Louis. On May 21, 1927, Lindbergh landed in Paris, where he was mobbed by spectators. He went on to win awards and acclaim from all of Europe and the U.S., the *New York Times* paying him $250,000 for his story. Lindbergh himself goes on to write a book about the flight. He and his plane "The Spirit of St. Louis" toured the U.S. upon their return and he became a national hero.

Lindbergh later married writer Anne Morrow in 1929, but in 1932 they suffered tragedy when their first child was kidnapped and killed. This eventually led to the development of what are now known as the "Lindbergh Laws," whereby interstate kidnapping is considered a federal crime. The Lindberghs then moved to Europe, where Charles helped a French surgeon invent an artificial heart. Returning to the U.S., Lindbergh served as an advisor to many aeronautical organizations and committees but during World War II his anti-war sentiments brought him into conflict with President Franklin Delano Roosevelt. After the war he continued his consultant work, and won numerous aviation awards--and the Pulitzer Prize for his autobiography, *The Spirit of St. Louis.*

Big Game Hunter

Big game hunters are skilled trackers and hunters who earn their livings leading safaris for wealthy sportsmen clients. Most are specialized in one part of the world such as the Canadian woods, African plains, or other. Although the great white hunter is the quintessential type, others may be simply local Indians who escort hunters through the backwoods of the Yukon in search of moose or bear.

EARNINGS: Lower middle class to Upper middle class.

CONTACTS AND CONNECTIONS: Local government officials and game wardens, past clients (which may include a celebrity or two).

SKILLS: Bargain, Firearms, First Aid, Hide, Jump, Knife, Listen, Natural History, Navigate, Other Language, Sneak, Track.

SPECIAL: Big game hunters stay cool when charged by large animals (even monsters). Calculate sanity losses as usual but the investigator does not suffer any adverse effects until after the incident is resolved.

Mountain Climber

Mountain climbing as a sport became popular in the 19th century. Most climbers are weekend and vacation sportsman; only a few have the reputations needed to attract the financing required for major climbs.

By the 1920s all the major American and Alpine peaks have been conquered. After lengthy negotiations with the Tibetans, climbers have finally been granted access to the highest peaks of the Himalayas. Regular assaults on Mt. Everest, the last unconquered peak in the world, are routinely covered by radio and newspapers. Expeditions in 1921, 1922, and 1924 all failed to reach the summit and resulted in the deaths of thirteen people.

EARNINGS: Lower middle class or better. Most climbers have separate incomes.

CONTACTS AND CONNECTIONS: Other climbers, park rangers, foreign governments, patrons.

SKILLS: Climb, First Aid, Jump, Listen, Navigate, Other Language, Photography, Roping, Track, plus possible employment skills.

SPECIAL: Add +1 to STR and +1 to CON. Climbers never suffer from a fear of heights unless specifically struck by a phobia.

Deep-Sea Diver

Deep-sea divers work as sponge gatherers, salvage divers, and even treasure hunters. The U.S. Navy maintains trained diving teams and it is possible that an investigator learned his occupation in the service. Tarpon Springs, Florida, is home to a flourishing sponge trade. Sponge boats--many of them owned by the large Greek community--sail out every day, sending down divers to find and collect sponges from the bottom.

EARNINGS: Upper Lower to Middle class.

CONTACTS AND CONNECTIONS: Coast Guard, smugglers.

SKILLS: Diving, Mechanical Repair, Natural History (Marine), Pilot Boat, Spot Hidden, Swim.

SPECIAL: +1 to CON. Add 20 bonus points to Spot Hidden.

Big Game Hunter Frank Buck (1884-1950)

Buck is the archetypal big game hunter. Born in Gainesville, Texas, his first expedition, in 1911, took him to Malaya and Singapore. Later safaris carried him around the world in search of wild animals which he captured alive and sold to zoos and circuses. All told, he captured more than 25,000 specimens in his career, including a man-eating tiger and the largest king cobra on record. He wrote of his experiences in books such as *Bring 'Em Back Alive* (1931) and later went on to make films.

Explorer Roald Amundsen (1872-1928)

Amundsen is a polar explorer, famous for discovering the South Pole in 1911 and the Northwest Passage in 1906. Later, from 1918 to 1920 he navigates the Northeast Passage. Amundsen was born in Oslo, Norway, and later joined the army. An expert navigator, he made many sea and air voyages between 1897-1928. In 1910 he had planned to be the first to reach the North Pole, but upon learning that Admiral Robert Peary had just reached it, turned his attention to the South Pole instead. He and his companions reached the Pole in December of 1911, beating British explorer Robert F. Scott's team by four weeks. Scott's bad luck turned to tragedy when his team froze to death during their return.

Amundsen made a dirigible flight over the North Pole with American Lincoln Ellsworth and the Italian General Umberto Nobile in 1926, mere days after Admiral Richard E. Byrd's solo flight. Amundsen perished in 1928, after setting out in a plane to search for Nobile, whose north polar expedition had been lost for several weeks. Nobile is later rescued.

Prospector

Though the days of the California Gold Rush and the Nevada Comstock Lode are long gone, the independent prospector is still a feature of the American West. Roaming the mountains, they endlessly search for the big strike that will make them rich. In these days oil may be as good as gold.

EARNINGS: Pauper to Lower class.

CONTACTS AND CONNECTIONS: Few--local, if any.

SKILLS: Climb, First Aid, Geology, History, Jump, Natural History, Navigate, Spot Hidden.

SPECIAL: +1 to STR and +1 to CON.

Treasure Hunter

A breed similar to prospectors, treasure-hunters also look to make the big strike. More common to the East where stories of buried pirate treasure and sunken ships filled with Spanish gold abound, a few in the West still search for the fabled golden cities sought by the Conquistadors. Most treasure hunting requires a team and serious financial backing. The necessary diving, digging, or other equipment can be expensive.

EARNINGS: Pauper and higher, depending on your luck.

CONTACTS AND CONNECTIONS: Investors, fellow treasure hunters, local governments, foreign governments, Coast Guard, local law officials.

SKILLS: Bargain, Climb, Drive Auto, Electrical Repair, History, Jump, Mechanical Repair, Persuade, Pilot Aircraft, Pilot Boat, Spot Hidden.

SPECIAL: Add 20 points to Spot Hidden.

Arts, Creative

CREATIVE ARTISTS INCLUDE writers, painters, and others. Artists often become investigators due to their creative efforts, suffering dreams or other visions that lead them to mysterious secrets. Many artists have created dark and eerie works, inspired by unknown sources, or know of artists who have had that experience.

Creative artists can pursue their own visions, working free lance, or be employed in a more commercial role, working for advertising companies or other.

Architect

Architects are usually college trained and familiar with some aspects of engineering. Junior architects employed by large firms find that getting supplier bids on 2000 doorknobs is part of their job. Others try and go it alone, working out of their house or a small office. Few manage to sell the grandiose designs they all nurse.

EARNINGS: Lower Middle to Upper Middle class.

CONTACTS AND CONNECTIONS: Local building and city engineering departments, construction firms.

SKILLS: Accounting, Art, Bargain, Credit Rating, English, Library Use, Persuade, Psychology.

SPECIAL: Special skill of Architectural History, 1D20+40 points.

Architect Frank Lloyd Wright (1869-1959)

In a career spanning more than sixty years, Frank Lloyd Wright designed over six hundred buildings and was hailed as one of the world's great architects. He was born in Wisconsin, and attended--but did not graduate from--the University of Wisconsin. In 1887 Wright secured a job as a draftsman and designer in the Chicago office of the famed architect Louis Sullivan. After six years as Sullivan's pupil, Wright went out on his own, designing many homes in and around Chicago. Here he developed what he termed "Prairie Style" homes: long, single-story buildings with interior rooms freely connected to each other without restricting doorways between. In 1911 he built his own home, Taliesin (Welsh for Shining Brow), in Spring Green, Wisconsin. In the 1930s he continued to experiment with new building styles, inventing such modern staples as the carport. In 1932 Wright founded The Taliesin Fellowship, an architectural school in Spring Green. He built a second home, Taliesin West, in Phoenix, Arizona, in 1938. Among the many public buildings designed by Wright is the Guggenheim Museum in New York City. He wrote a number of books and magazines on architecture as well as *An Autobiography* in 1943.

Painter

Designer

Designers work in all fields: fashion, stage, furniture design, light fixtures, etc. The investigator's particular specialty might influence the choice of skills.

EARNINGS: Lower Middle to Upper Middle class.

CONTACTS AND CONNECTIONS: Advertising, stage, furnishings, architectural, other.

SKILLS: Accounting, Art, Bargain, Electrical Repair, Mechanical Repair, Photography, Psychology.

Painter/Sculptor

The plastic arts are always popular but materials are expensive and sales infrequent. Many artists work in advertising firms drawing pictures of washing machines and automobiles.

EARNINGS: Commercial artists are Lower Middle to Middle class.

CONTACTS AND CONNECTIONS: Art galleries, critics, patrons, the advertising industry.

SKILLS: Art, Bargain, History, Library Use, Persuade, Photography, Psychology.

SPECIAL: All artists have a beginning Art History skill of 1D20+40 points.

Author Ernest Hemingway (1899-1961)

Ernest Hemingway was an immensely popular writer of novels and stories dealing with men and women driven to despair by a violent and uncaring world. He was born in Illinois, but grew up in nearby Michigan. An ambulance driver in the Great War, he was badly wounded in Italy when only eighteen. After the war he moved to Paris, where his war and post-war experiences with other expatriate Americans serve as the basis for his novels *The Sun Also Rises* (1926) and *A Farewell to Arms* (1929). These novels help to define "the lost generation" that was currently coming of age in the post-war years.

Two collections of Hemingway's stories appeared during the 1920s: *In Our Time* (1925) and *Men Without Women* (1927). Hemingway went to Africa in the 1930s where he hunted big game. He later visited Spain and immersed himself in bull-fighting, and later still covered the Spanish Civil War as a war correspondent. His post-1920s works were not received with as much critical acclaim as his earlier works--with the exceptions of *For Whom the Bell Tolls* (1940) and *The Old Man and the Sea* (1952). The latter won the Nobel Prize for Literature in 1954. Seven years later, in poor health, Hemingway committed suicide.

Painter Salvador Dali (1904-1989)

Dali was born in Spain and given the name Salvador Felipe y Jacinto Dali y Domenech. Son of a prominent lawyer, he studied at the Academy of Fine Arts in Madrid intermittently from 1921-1926. Always a flamboyant figure, he was expelled from the academy and later briefly imprisoned under suspicion of being an anarchist. His first one-man show was held in Barcelona in 1925. His earlier works were influenced by the futurist and cubist painters, but in 1927 he moved to Paris, where he met Picasso. In 1929 he turned to the style for which he became famous: "surrealism." Dali also contributed to the screenplays of the bizarre surrealistic film maker, Luis Bunuel: *Un Chien Andalou* (1929) and *L'Age d'Or* (1931).

Photographer

Photography as an art form has been around a long time, but most photographers work for advertising firms or in portrait studios taking pictures of families. Others are employed in the newspaper and film industries.

EARNINGS: Lower Middle to Middle class.

CONTACTS AND CONNECTIONS: The advertising, news, and/or film industries, possibly film and camera manufacturers.

SKILLS: Accounting, Chemistry, Photography, Persuade, Physics, Psychology.

SPECIAL: Photographers have a Dark Room skill equal to their photography skill. Special emulsions capable of capturing invisible or alien creatures on film might be developed if successful Chemistry rolls are made.

Writer

A writer can be a struggling novelist, pulp hack, magazine author, scree'nplay writer, song lyricist, poet, a writer of advertising copy, or any combination of these.

EARNINGS: Writing ad copy brings a Lower Middle class income.

CONTACTS AND CONNECTIONS: Libraries, other writers, the publishing, advertising, and/or film industries.

SKILLS: Art, English, Fast Talk, Library Use, Other Language, Persuade, Psychology.

SPECIAL: Special skill of Literature History begins at 1D20+20 points.

Arts, Performing

Entertainer

A performing entertainer may be a singer, dancer, musician, comedian, ventriloquist, juggler, or other--or any combination of these different talents. New York's Broadway and off-Broadway stages are the pinnacle, but theatres are found in every large city. Vaudeville is nearly gone, but not quite dead, and many song-and-dance men still work this old circuit. Others go to Hollywood hoping to find a spot in the film industry.

EARNINGS: Upper Lower to Lower Middle class.

Jazz Musician

CONTACTS AND CONNECTIONS: Vaudeville, Broadway stage, film industry, and entertainment critics. Organized crime is very active in the entertainment industry.

SKILLS: Art(s), Disguise, English, Fast Talk, Persuade, Psychology.

SPECIAL: +1 to APP, and either +1 to DEX or 50 points to any applicable entertainment skills such as Dance, Sing, or others.

Musician, Jazz

Jazz musicians work in small combos and dance orchestras in large and medium-sized cities and towns. A few musicians living in large cities like Chicago or New York find steady work in their hometown but most spend significant amounts of time on the road, touring by bus, auto, and train.

EARNINGS: Lower Class. Cash, by the night.

CONTACTS AND CONNECTIONS: Club owners, musicians' union, organized crime, street scene, drug pushers.

SKILLS: Art(s), Bargain, Fast Talk, Listen, Persuade, Psychology.

Musician, Legitimate

Legitimate musicians are trained in schools and colleges. They strive for steady salaried employment in civic orchestras.

EARNINGS: Lower Middle class.

CONTACTS AND CONNECTIONS: Other musicians, the musicians' union, patrons.

SKILLS: Accounting, Art(s), Bargain, Listen, Persuade, Psychology.

Stage Actor

Although the theatre center of the U.S. is in New York City, there are major stages in most cities across the country. Touring companies travel by train, presenting new plays as well as classics by Shakespeare and others. Some companies spend considerable amounts of time

Entertainer Will Rogers (1879-1935)

Will Rogers was a cowboy, a star of stage and screen, a writer, and a homespun philosopher. Born in Indian territory in Oklahoma to parents of partial Indian descent, Rogers briefly attended military school in Missouri before heading to Texas in 1898, seeking work as a cowhand. His wanderlust later led him to Argentina and South Africa, where he worked in a Wild West show. Rogers first performed on an American stage in New York City in 1905, but gained real fame as part of the Ziegfeld Follies in 1916. He later appeared in motion pictures such as *A Connecticut Yankee* (1931) and *State Fair* (1933).

Rogers' newspaper column, where he told down-to-earth stories and dispensed philosophy, was also enormously popular (on stage, this patter is accompanied by elaborate rope tricks). Over three hundred newspapers carried his column, where he wittily commented on current events. In 1926 President Calvin Coolidge sent Rogers to Europe as America's "Ambassador of Good Will," which Rogers drily commented on in *Letters of a Self-Made Diplomat to His President* (1927). Other books included *The Cowboy Philosopher on Prohibition* (1919) and *There's Not a Bathing Suit in Russia* (1927). Rogers was married to an Arkansas schoolteacher and had four children. He was killed in 1935 in a plane crash near Point Barrow, Alaska, along with famed pilot Wiley Post.

Composer Bela Bartok (1881-1945)

Bartok, a Hungarian, was destined to become one of the most important composers of the 20th century. His works include six string quartets, the opera *Duke Bluebeard's Castle* (1911), numerous concertos for piano and orchestra, and the incredible *Mikrokosmos* (1926-1937). Bartok began studying music at the age of five and soon became an accomplished pianist and composer, eventually teaching piano at the Royal Hungarian Academy of Music in Budapest. Bartok later toured as a concert pianist, visiting the U.S. in 1927 and in 1928. During World War II, he moved to New York City and joined the staff of Columbia University.

Actor John Barrymore (1882-1942)

Born John Sydney Blythe, Barrymore was the younger brother of his acting siblings, Ethel and Lionel, and descended from one of America's most famous theatre families. By the 1920s, John is the most highly regarded Shakespearean actor of his time, well known for his stage portrayal of Hamlet. Barrymore carried his successful stage presence to motion pictures making, among others, a silent version of *Dr. Jekyll and Mr. Hyde* (1920), a talkie version of *Moby Dick* (1930), and a chilling turn as the title character in *Svengali* (1931). He later became a popular radio actor as well.

working outside the U.S., touring Canada, Hawaii, Australia, and other places.

Many stage actors have a background in the classics and, considering themselves "legitimate," look down upon the commercial efforts of the film industry.

EARNINGS: Upper Lower to Lower Middle class.

CONTACTS AND CONNECTIONS: Theatre industry, newspaper critics, actor's guild.

SKILLS: Art, Disguise, English, Fast Talk, Persuade, Psychology.

SPECIAL: +1 to APP. Actors are skilled at disguising their emotions (when they wish to) and are difficult to analyze with Psychology. Lies and hidden motivations escape detection as the actor weaves a false reality for himself and others.

Stage Hand

Stage hands work behind the scenes, moving props, working lights, providing sound effects, and constructing and painting sets. Most, if not all, are aspiring actors awaiting their big chance. Aside from their regular chores they also play the parts of extras and often understudy for larger roles.

EARNINGS: Pauper to Upper Lower class.

CONTACTS AND CONNECTIONS: Theatre industry, actor's guild.

SKILLS: Art(s), English, Fast Talk, Disguise, Persuade, Psychology.

Film Star

Movie stars and the film industry have captured the interest of America. Many stars are made 'overnight' and most of them lead flashy, high-profile lives.

Many careers are lost with the introduction of talkies in the latter part of the decade. With the addition of dialogue, the arm-waving histrionics of silent actors give way to more subtle characterizations. John Garfield and Francis X. Bushman are forgotten for new stars such as Gary Cooper and Joan Crawford.

EARNINGS: Pauper to Wealthy.

CONTACTS AND CONNECTIONS: The film industry, newspaper critics, organized crime, actor's guild.

SKILLS: Art, Bargain, Disguise, English, Fast Talk, Persuade, Psychology.

SPECIAL: +1 to APP.

Stunt Man

The film industry employs many stunt man to simulate falls from buildings, auto crashes, and other catastrophes. There is no stunt man organization nor any regulation of the industry. Accidents are frequent.

EARNINGS: Upper Lower class.

CONTACTS AND CONNECTIONS: The film industry, various explosive and pyrotechnic firms, free lance inventors.

SKILLS: Climb, Disguise, Dodge, Drive Automobile, Electrical Repair, First Aid, Fist/Punch, Grapple, Head Butt, Jump, Kick, Mechanical Repair, Pilot Aircraft, Pilot Boat, Ride, Swim, Throw.

SPECIAL: +1 to CON and +1 to DEX. Subtract 1D3 points from any damage caused by an accidental fall. Drive and Piloting skills allow the stunt man to perform stunts or safely crash these types of vehicles.

Film Crew

Film crews are more specialized than theater stage crews and include carpenters, electricians, cameramen, costu-

Film Star Lon Chaney (1883-1930)

Lon Chaney made a legendary career out of playing deformed villains and monsters in silent films. Born in Colorado Springs, Chaney learned to communicate with his deaf mute parents using gestures--a practice which proved useful in his later film career. He quit school in the fifth grade to become a tour guide at Pikes Peak, later working as a stage hand in the theater where his older brother John performed. He appeared in productions of Gilbert and Sullivan operas and on the vaudeville stage in Chicago, where he was enough of a success that he was able to join Universal studios as a bit player.

The Miracle Man (1919) was the first in a series of roles that would make Lon Chaney famous. In this film Chaney appeared as the twisted Frog, a horribly crippled man who nonetheless captured the audience's sympathy. In subsequent roles like *The Hunchback of Notre Dame* (1923) and *The Phantom of the Opera* (1925) he delighted and terrified audiences with his horribly deformed yet pathetic characters. He became known as "The Man of a Thousand Faces," creating his own unique and often painful makeup devices. (He later wrote the Encyclopedia Britannica entry on the subject of film makeup.) In 1930 his only sound feature was released--a remake of his earlier silent hit *The Unholy Three*. Chaney played three roles in this film, including a man masquerading as an old woman. The film and its star received critical acclaim but a month later Chaney was dead of throat cancer. His son, born Creighton Chaney, later changed his name to Lon Chaney Jr. and made his own career in horror films.

mers, and many others. Unions are already making inroads in a film industry earning enough money to easily concede to most of their demands. Unlike their counterparts on the stage, members of film crews are rarely aspiring actors.

EARNINGS: Lower Middle class.

CONTACTS AND CONNECTIONS: The film industry, associated unions.

SKILLS: Art(s), Climb, Drive Automobile, Electrical Repair, Mechanical Repair, Photography.

Talent Agent

Agents work for authors, artists, actors, producers and others, either selling the artist, or his works.

EARNINGS: Commission, Lower class and higher.

CONTACTS AND CONNECTIONS: Publishing industry, film industry, others.

SKILLS: Accounting, Bargain, Fast Talk, Law, Persuade, Psychology.

SPECIAL: Impervious to most Fast Talk.

Dancer Isadora Duncan (1878-1927)

Isadora Duncan is a pioneer in the development of modern dance. Born in San Francisco, she eschewed traditional ballet disciplines, preferring natural movements in her dances, which she performed barefoot, dressed in a Greek tunic. She became popular in the U.S. and abroad, and started many dance schools, all of them short-lived. Duncan wrote an autobiography, *My Life* and, later, a collection of essays *The Art of the Dance*. She was killed in a freak auto accident in France in 1927.

Athletics

ATHLETICS HAVE BEEN popular in the U.S. since the latter part of the 19th century. Organized amateur competition was long popular with local aristocracy, politicians, and other social types, but by the 1920s many of these amateur athletics clubs have evolved into social organizations that have but little to do with athletics.

Professional sports, long regarded as somewhat lower class, have become, with the development of the mass media, big business. Baseball is "the national pastime" featuring two leagues and an annual World Series; Babe Ruth earns more money than the president. Pro football is nowhere near as popular but is lately starting to at least draw as much attention as college football. Basketball leagues come and go as rules and regulations are continually sorted out and modified. Hockey is something done by Canadians.

Boxing is very popular, as well as professional wrestling. Professional golf and tennis have gained in popularity, due in part to the fact that these games can be enjoyed by the common man. Polo remains popular mostly with the upper crust.

Baseball Player

Professional Athlete

You play on a professional baseball, football, or basketball team. This may be a major league team with a reasonable, regular salary and national attention or--particularly in the case of baseball--one of many minor league teams, some of them owned and operated by major league owners. The latter pay barely enough to keep players fed and on the team. In any case, professional athletes spend a considerable amount of time on the road in buses and on trains.

EARNINGS: Lower class for minor leaguers, Lower Middle class and above for the majors.

CONTACTS AND CONNECTIONS: Sports personalities, sports writers, gamblers.

SKILLS: Block, Club (baseball bat), Dodge, Grapple, Head Butt, Jump, Kick, Spot Hidden, Throw.

SPECIAL: Add +1 to CON and +1 to either STR, SIZ, DEX, or movement rate. Subtract 2 from EDU

Boxer, Wrestler

Boxers and wrestlers are managed by individuals or small teams of managers and trainers, and possibly backed by outside interests. Professional boxers and wrestlers work and train full-time. They are usually locked into contracts. Amateur boxing competitions abound, a training ground for the pros.

EARNINGS: Lower class to Lower Middle class.

CONTACTS AND CONNECTIONS: Boxing promoters, sports writers, organized crime.

SKILLS: Block, Fist/Punch, Grapple, Dodge, Head Butt, Kick.

SPECIAL: Add +2 to CON, +1 to STR. Subtract 2 from EDU.

Tennis Pro

Most tennis players are from well-to-do families and more often than not from warmer climates where the sport can be played year round. A few pros tour the big money circuit, but most hold salaried positions at country clubs where they provide lessons to well-feathered club members.

EARNINGS: Lower Middle to Upper Middle class.

CONTACTS AND CONNECTIONS: Other tennis pros, sports writers, wealthy and/or influential club members (doctors, lawyers, judges, businessmen, etc.).

SKILLS: Bargain, Club (tennis racket), Credit Rating, Dodge, Jump, Persuade, Psychology, Spot Hidden.

SPECIAL: +1 to CON and +1 to DEX. Subtract 2 from EDU. A good build and a fine tan can add as much as +2 to APP, particularly when dealing with members of the opposite sex.

Golf Pro

Professional golfers are often from warm climates where the links are available year round. Most grew up working as caddies and/or grounds keepers, spending all their spare time golfing. Most golf pros hold steady jobs at privately-owned golf courses, giving lessons, socializing with club members, etc.

EARNINGS: Middle to Upper Middle class.

CONTACTS AND CONNECTIONS: Other pros, sports writers, wealthy and/or influential club members (doctors, lawyers, judges, businessmen, etc.)

SKILLS: Bargain, Club (golf club), Credit Rating, Persuade, Psychology, Spot Hidden.

SPECIAL: +1 to CON, -2 to EDU.

Baseball Player Babe Ruth (1895–1948)

George Herman Ruth, better known as "The Babe," "Bambino," or "The Sultan of Swat," was baseball's first and greatest slugger. He was born in Baltimore, where he attended catholic school. There a teacher noted his baseball skills and helped him begin his career. In 1914 Ruth joins the Boston Red Sox as a pitcher, a position where he earned some success. When the Sox traded him to the New York Yankees he played mostly in the outfield. In New York Ruth honed his slugging skills, hitting a record-setting sixty home runs in 1927. When the Yankees built a new stadium it quickly became known as "The House That Ruth Built." He played in ten World Series and twice (in 1926 and 1928) hit three home runs in a single World Series game. Ruth's personality and slugging skill made him the most popular player in baseball. In 1934 Ruth left the Yankees and played with the Boston Braves for one year before retiring from baseball. He was named to the Hall of Fame in 1936, and died of cancer twelve years later. His record of 714 career home runs stood for over forty years.

Boxer Jack Dempsey (1895-1983)

Born in Manassa, Colorado, Dempsey started boxing in mining camps in 1912, earning himself the nickname the "Manassa Mauler." Dempsey gained the heavyweight title in 1918 by knocking out Jess Willard, and successfully defended it three times before losing it to Gene Tunney in 1926. In a rematch with Tunney in 1927, Dempsey knocked Tunney down but failed to go to a neutral corner. The ensuing "long count" became infamous in boxing circles, as upwards of fifteen seconds passed before the referee reached the count of "Nine." Tunney got up and went on to win a much-disputed ten-round decision.

Track and Field

This includes all the various running, jumping, and throwing events. There are only a few professional events in the world and most competitors are amateurs.

EARNINGS: Pauper.

CONTACTS AND CONNECTIONS: Amateur athletic world, sports writers.

SKILLS: Climb, Dodge, Jump, Other Language, Throw, plus possible employment skills.

SPECIAL: Add +1 to CON, and either +1 to STR or movement speed.

Acrobat

Acrobats may be either amateur athletes competing in staged meets--possibly even the Olympics--or professional acrobats employed by circuses and carnivals. Some have begun amateurs and later turned pro.

EARNINGS: Lower to Lower Middle class.

CONTACTS AND CONNECTIONS: Amateur athletic circles, sports writers, circuses and carnivals.

SKILLS: Bargain, Climb, Dodge, Jump, Other Language, Throw, plus possible employment skills.

SPECIAL: +1 to STR and +1 to DEX, or +2 to DEX.

Swimmer/Diver

Most swimmers have had access to pools or suitable lakes while growing up; quite often they are the children of university athletic coaches. Most swimmers are amateurs; there are no professional swimming meets.

EARNINGS: Pauper.

CONTACTS AND CONNECTIONS: Amateur athletic world, sports writers.

SKILLS: Other Language, Swim, plus possible employment skills.

SPECIAL: Swimmers add +1 to their CON and +1 to their swim movement speed. Unless conditions dictate otherwise (freezing temperatures, strong currents, undertow, waves, etc.), accomplished swimmers are nearly impervious to drowning, capable of treading water nearly effortlessly for hours.

Manager/Coach

Usually ex-athletes too old to compete, managers and coaches direct teams, conduct practices, and plan strategies. Coaches of popular college football teams are some of the most well-known celebrities in sports, and highly-paid. Trainers of gymnasts and others become father-figures to their most gifted athletes, often forming long-lasting, personal relationships.

EARNINGS: Upper Lower to Upper Middle class.

CONTACTS AND CONNECTIONS: Athletic circles, sports writers, wealthy and influential alumnae.

SKILLS: Accounting, Bargain, Block, Dodge, Fast Talk, First Aid, Head Butt, Kick, Persuade, Psychology.

SPECIAL: +1 to SIZ.

Swimmer Johnny Weismuller (1904-1984)

Johnny Weismuller set over sixty American and world swimming records in the 1920s, breaking the 100-yard free style record five times between 1922-1927. He won five Olympic gold medals, three in 1924 and two in 1928. In the 1930s Weismuller went on to play the lead role in a dozen Tarzan films for MGM and RKO, beginning with *Tarzan the Ape Man* (1932) and ending with *Tarzan and the Mermaids* (1948). For many, Weismuller's depiction of the Lord of the Apes was the definitive one. Weismuller was born in Windber, Pennsylvania.

Baseball Commissioner Judge Kenesaw Mountain Landis (1866-1944)

Landis, born in Millville, Ohio, was an Illinois judge who later became the first commissioner of professional baseball. He was a well-respected U.S. District Court judge in northern Illinois for several years. One of his most famous cases resulted in fines levied on the Standard Oil Company totalling over twenty-nine million dollars. His fairness and incorruptibility led to his appointment as baseball commissioner. This followed the 1919 "Black Sox" scandal, in which the World Series was fixed by gamblers, allowing the Cincinnati Reds to defeat the Chicago White Sox. Landis steered the game away from further scandals, and was eventually elected to the Baseball Hall of Fame in 1944.

Trainer

Trainers are charged with the conditioning and physical well-being of the athletes. They are usually employed by college or professional teams.

EARNINGS: Lower to Upper Lower class.

CONTACTS AND CONNECTIONS: Athletic world.

SKILLS: Fast Talk, First Aid, Medicine, Persuade, Pharmacy, Psychology.

SPECIAL: Trainers enjoy a special skill called Sports Medicine beginning at 1D20+40 points. In game terms it can be used to splint, brace, or otherwise repair an injured limb so that it remains at least semi-functional. This can be used to put an investigator with a sprained ankle back on his feet.

Business

BUSINESS BOOMS THROUGH most of the 1920s, a period of unprecedented growth in the U.S. Note that the descriptions below pertain to conditions before the Wall Street Crash of 1929. Once the Great Depression sets in, many things change.

Most lower and middle level business occupations offer but little chance to come into contact with strange mysteries. At the higher levels, however, individuals sometimes become investigators after being asked to help finance expeditions or research, or through some antiquity they have collected.

Company Officer/Executive

These are high-paying positions in large national and multi-national corporations. Chairman of the Board is usually the highest title, followed by one or more Presidents and often near-countless vice-presidents. Other executives are titled managers, and wait impatiently for promotion.

Occupations are available in any manufacturing industry--the auto industry being one of the largest-- or light and power, banking, or even the news and film industries.

Although bachelors are not infrequent, most executive types are family men with wives and children. It is often expected of them.

EARNINGS: Upper Middle class to Wealthy.

CONTACTS AND CONNECTIONS: Business and finance worlds, old college connections, Masons or other fraternal groups, local and federal governments. Advertising budgets may afford you leverage in the newspaper and magazine industry.

SKILLS: Accounting, Bargain, Credit Rating, English, Fast Talk, Persuade, Psychology.

SPECIAL: Add 20 bonus points (35 for a company officer) to Credit Rating.

Stock Broker

Brokers are licensed by the state and approved by the exchange. You may work out of an office or right on the trading floors of one of New York's big boards, Chicago's Commodities Market, or San Francisco's Pacific Stock Exchange.

EARNINGS: Upper Middle class to Wealthy.

CONTACTS AND CONNECTIONS: Business and finance worlds, hungry investors.

Company Executive

SKILLS: Accounting, Bargain, Credit Rating, English, Fast Talk, Persuade, Psychology.

SPECIAL: Add 30 points to your Credit Rating.

Auto Tycoon Henry Ford (1863-1947)

Born on a farm in Michigan, Henry Ford was a pioneer of American manufacturing. He worked as a machinist in Detroit while experimenting with engines and in 1896 completed his first crude automobile. In 1903 he started the Ford Motor Company, at first producing slow, expensive models. Developing mass-production techniques allowed Ford to lower the cost on his cars, and by 1927 he had sold over fifteen million of his Model Ts.

Ford is generous with his success, and in 1914 began sharing profits with his employees. He also lowered working hours and raised the minimum wage considerably. These and other practices brought friction from his stockholders, so Ford bought them out in 1919, ensuring that his family would control the company unimpeded even after his death. Though initially opposed to U.S. involvement in the Great War, Ford later turned his factories to aiding the war effort. He later developed the V-8 engine, and became involved in many philanthropic interests, including the Ford Foundation. Established in 1936, the Ford Foundation was the world's largest philanthropic organization.

Accountant

Although the accounting department is essential to any business endeavor it is usually outside the mainstream of the company. Few, if any, are ever promoted out of Accounting.

EARNINGS: Upper Lower to Middle class.

CONTACTS AND CONNECTIONS: Other accountants.

SKILLS: Accounting, Accounting, Accounting, Credit Rating.

Clerk

The lowest level white-collar position. Clerks are habitually underpaid and the work is drudgery. They hope to gain a managerial position someday.

EARNINGS: Upper Lower to Lower Middle class.

CONTACTS AND CONNECTIONS: Other office workers.

SKILLS: Accounting, Bargain, Credit Rating, English, Fast Talk, Persuade, Psychology.

Secretary

A position that ranges from high-paid private executive assistant to the typing pool. Men occasionally serve at the higher positions but the lower levels are almost exclusively female.

EARNINGS: Upper Lower to Middle class.

CONTACTS AND CONNECTIONS: Other office workers.

Business Owner Howard Hughes (1905-1976)

Howard Hughes was a success in a number of business ventures, ranging from aviation, to motion picture production, to tool manufacturing. Hughes was born in Houston, Texas. Orphaned at the age of seventeen, he quit school to take over his father's Hughes Tool Company in Houston. In the early 1930s Hughes began producing motion pictures, among them *Hell's Angels* (1930), *The Front Page* (1931), and *Scarface* (1932). His films introduced such cinematic legends as Jean Harlow, Paul Muni, and Jane Russell.

An avid flyer, he set several aviation speed records in the late 1930s, and started Hughes Aircraft Company in Culver City, California. In the 1940s he became involved with RKO Pictures, buying controlling interest and then the company itself. Later he sold, repurchased, and finally sold the company again in 1954; he stayed on RKO's board of directors until 1957. Always a recluse, Hughes disappeared from the public eye in the 1950s. After his death in 1976 it was revealed that Hughes had been in terrible health for many years due to the poor diet and living conditions he had forced upon himself.

SKILLS: Accounting, Credit Rating, English, Fast Talk, Persuade, Psychology.

SPECIAL: Special skills include such things as Typing and Shorthand, the latter of particular use in certain situations.

Switchboard Operator

Another position held almost exclusively by women. Company phone systems are large and incoming calls must be routed to the proper party by hand. Short patch cords are used to connect incoming calls with the proper office. A pleasant phone voice is considered a plus.

Although the phone company still employs many operators, automatic switching equipment is already being installed which handles the vast majority of local calls.

EARNINGS: Upper Lower to Lower Middle class.

CONTACTS AND CONNECTIONS: Other office workers. Also, operators can listen in on phone calls at will. They usually know more of the intimate details of a corporation or office than anyone else.

SKILLS: Credit Rating, English, Fast Talk, Listen, Persuade, Psychology.

Salesman

An integral part of many businesses, salesmen maintain small offices at company headquarters but spend much of their time on the outside meeting clients, buying lunches, and sharing drinks. Salesmen are likely to change employment from one company to another, almost effortlessly. Some sell product, others services; some sell advertising space in newspapers and magazines, or on radio broadcasts.

EARNINGS: Lower Middle to Upper Middle class.

CONTACTS AND CONNECTIONS: Particular to the specific area of business or industry the salesman is involved with.

SKILLS: Accounting, Bargain, Credit Rating, Fast Talk, Persuade, Psychology.

SPECIAL: Salesmen are nearly impervious to Fast Talk or Persuade, and Psychology usually reveals little about them other than a desire to sell their product or service. Once the salesman is better known to a person, Psychology is more effective.

Traveling Salesman

It is the decade of the entrepreneur and the traveling salesman is a part of everyday life. Some work directly for companies and others on consignment, but most live and die by commission. Some are restricted to certain territories but others are free to roam and seek out prospects wherever they might be found. Brushes, vacuum cleaners, and encyclopedias are only a few of the many items currently sold door-to-door.

EARNINGS: Upper Lower to Lower Middle class.

CONTACTS AND CONNECTIONS: Few.

SKILLS: Accounting, Bargain, Drive Automobile, Fast Talk, Navigate, Persuade, Psychology.

SPECIAL: +1 to CON. Traveling salesmen are generally impervious to Fast Talk and Persuade. Psychology is mostly ineffective, unless the salesman is well-known to the person.

Small Business Owner

Small businesses employ a dozen or more people and are usually built up by the owner from scratch. A small manufacturing plant, a print shop, a machining or plating

Investor Joseph Kennedy (1888-1969)

Joseph Patrick Kennedy was one of the richest and most powerful businessmen in America. Kennedy was born in Boston and graduated from Harvard. In 1913, at the age of twenty-five, Joe Kennedy took control of a Boston bank and thus became the youngest bank president in the country. A year later, he married Rose Fitzgerald, the daughter of Boston's mayor. The Kennedys had four sons, one of whom died in World War II while the others went on to become senators and a president. Joe Kennedy himself became embroiled in politics in 1934 when President Franklin Delano Roosevelt appointed him to the Securities and Exchange Commission. He later served as chairman of that organization, and also of the U.S. Maritime Commission (1937), and was ambassador to great Britain from 1937-1940. Much of Joe Kennedy's fortune was made via shrewd investments, but illegal bootlegging activities are also said to have helped fill Kennedy coffers.

outlet, design company, etc.--all qualify. Although perhaps successful and monied, the small business owner's background is usually middle class, at best.

This character knows how to do every job in the place, probably better than most of his employees.

EARNINGS: Middle to Upper class.

CONTACTS AND CONNECTIONS: Those within the realm of his particular business and finance needs: bankers, suppliers, customers, etc.

SKILLS: Accounting, Bargain, Credit Rating, Fast Talk, Persuade, Psychology.

SPECIAL: Add 20 points to Credit Rating; add an extra 30 points to any skill or skills applicable to your business, due to your wide experience and background.

Shopkeeper

The owner of a small shop, market, or restaurant is a self-employed person with few, if any, employees. Family members often work the business, and the owner usually lives in an apartment behind or above the store. In the 1920s many women open their own hairdressing and millinery shops.

EARNINGS: Upper Lower to Middle class.

CONTACTS AND CONNECTIONS: Local residents, local police, local government.

SKILLS: Accounting, Bargain, Credit Rating, Fast Talk, Persuade, Psychology.

SPECIAL: Add 20 points to Credit Rating.

Barber

Barbers are licensed by the state--a practice dating back to the days when barbers were also surgeons. During the 1920s barbers vigorously campaign against female owned and operated "hair-dressing salons" where hair is being cut without the requisite licenses.

EARNINGS: Upper Lower to Lower Middle class.

CONTACTS AND CONNECTIONS: Depends on barber's particular clientele.

SKILLS: Accounting, Bargain, Credit Rating, Fast Talk, Persuade, Psychology, Straight Razor.

Clergy

MEMBERS OF THE CLERGY are exposed to odd mysteries more often than many other occupational types. Parishioners confessing crimes or sins, seeking aid, or asking for an explanation of their strange dreams often lead a member of the clergy to life as an investigator. Additionally, anomalies are often stumbled upon during the course of researching old tomes, or when on mission in some far corner of the globe. Some have even been drawn in when called upon to perform an exorcism, or rid a person or house of a curse.

Catholic Priest

Priests are celibate, and answer directly to the hierarchy of the Catholic Church and the Pope. The Church usually assigns priests to their respective parishes, or sends them on missions. Priests may rise through the ranks of bishop,

Priest

> **Priest Patrick J. Hayes (1867-1938)**
>
> Hayes was a cardinal in the Roman Catholic Church in New York City, where he was born. He was ordained in 1892 and in 1919 was appointed archbishop of New York. He helped create many New York Catholic charities, for which he developed a loyal following both in the church and among the people. Hayes was made a cardinal in 1924.

archbishop, and cardinal. Many are trained in professional skills, acting as doctors, lawyers, and scholars.

EARNINGS: Upper Lower to Upper Middle class.

CONTACTS AND CONNECTIONS: Church hierarchy, local congregation, community leaders. Priests bear witness to confessions and though they are not at liberty to divulge such secrets, they are free to act upon them.

SKILLS: Accounting, Bargain, Credit Rating, English, Latin, Library Use, Occult, Other Language, Persuade, Psychology.

Special: Add 20 bonus points to Credit Rating.

Rabbi

Rabbis are scholars and advisors, trained in the Hebrew faith. They usually practice in the neighborhood where they grew up.

EARNINGS: Lower class to Upper Middle class.

CONTACTS AND CONNECTIONS: Jewish scholars, the local Jewish community.

SKILLS: English, Credit Rating, Hebrew, History, Library Use, Occult, Other Language, Persuade, Psychology.

SPECIAL: Add 30 bonus points to Credit Rating.

Protestant Minister

Protestant ministers run a range of types from the robed priests of the Episcopal Church, to the suited professionals of the Unitarians, to the fire-and-brimstone preachers of evangelist faiths.

EARNINGS: Lower Middle to Upper Middle class. Some are full-time salaried, others serve without compensation.

CONTACTS AND CONNECTIONS: Specific church hierarchy, congregation, local community leaders.

SKILLS: Accounting, Bargain, Credit Rating, English, Library Use, Persuade, Psychology.

SPECIAL: Add 10 bonus points to Credit Rating.

Missionary

Most often a Catholic Priest or Protestant Minister, missionaries visit remote corners of the globe dispensing the word of God to the unfortunate primitives. Mormons are also called upon to perform missions, but these are often in urban areas including parts of the U.S. Being sent on a two-year mission to Los Angeles is not impossible.

Laymen also serve as missionaries. They are often professionals: doctors or other skilled types.

EARNINGS: Pauper to Lower Middle class.

CONTACTS AND CONNECTIONS: Church hierarchy, foreign officials.

SKILLS: Anthropology, Bargain, English, Occult, Other Language, Persuade, Psychology.

SPECIAL: +1 to CON.

Deacon/Elder

A deacon or other type of elder is a lay member of the church serving in an official capacity as an officer or director of church activities and business.

EARNINGS: Unpaid.

CONTACTS AND CONNECTIONS: Church hierarchy, the congregation, local business and community leaders.

Sister Aimee Semple McPherson (1890-1944)

Aimee Semple McPherson was born in Canada, destined to become one of the most popular evangelists of her day. Early in her career, McPherson worked as a missionary in Hong Kong with her husband, an evangelist named Robert Semple. When he died, she and her daughter returned to the U.S., where she toured the country performing very theatrical revival services, eventually becoming known as "Sister Aimee." A popular and vivacious figure, her services (performed both in person and on the radio) stressed salvation, the Second Coming of Christ, and divine healing. McPherson built a radio station, edited a magazine, and founded the International Church of the Foursquare Gospel (1927) and the Lighthouse of International Foursquare Evangelism Bible College. She built the Angelus Temple in Los Angeles in 1922. At the height of her career in the 1930s, Aimee Semple McPherson's gospel was taught in over two hundred missions across the country. She died from an overdose of barbiturates in 1944.

SKILLS: Accounting, Bargain, Credit Rating, Fast Talk, Persuade, Psychology, plus employment skills.

SPECIAL: Add 10 bonus points to Credit Rating.

Itinerant Preacher

Itinerants are usually dusty, ragged preachers traveling the country on foot, spreading the word of God on street corners and in parking lots. Many proclaim the forthcoming end of the world.

EARNINGS: Pauper to Lower class.

CONTACTS AND CONNECTIONS: Speaks with God.

SKILLS: Bargain, English, Fast Talk, Hide, Persuade, Psychology, Sneak.

SPECIAL: Most suffer a penalty of minus 20 sanity points from beginning current sanity but, being half-mad already, are usually impervious to the effects of temporary insanity--although they lose sanity points as normal.

Bible Salesman

Not restricting themselves to Bibles, these travelers spread the word of God through tracts, subscriptions, and other devices.

EARNINGS: Lower to Upper Lower class.

CONTACTS AND CONNECTIONS: Religious publishers.

SKILLS: Accounting, Bargain, Persuade, Psychology.

SPECIAL: +1 to CON.

Charismatic Cult Leader

America has always generated new religions, from the New England Transcendentalists to the Latter-Day Saints, as well as many others. During the 1920s any number of charismatic cult leaders emerge. Some espouse forms of Christianity while others incorporate Eastern mysticism and occult practices. These groups are particularly familiar to America's West Coast but are found all around the country in different forms. The southern Bible Belt supports many traveling tent shows featuring song, dance, and gospel revival.

EARNINGS: Upper Lower to Upper Middle class.

CONTACTS AND CONNECTIONS: Possibly movie stars, rich widows, others.

SKILLS: Accounting, Bargain, Credit Rating, Fast Talk, Persuade, Psychology.

SPECIAL: +1 to APP.

Criminals

PROHIBITION LED TO THE rise of organized crime. Ethnic street gangs took advantage of the ban on alcohol to corner the black market, warring with one another for the right to sell liquor and beer to a thirsty public.

Gangster

Gangsterism rose to prominence in the 1920s. Neighborhood ethnic gangs who had heretofore limited their activities to local protection schemes and small gambling rackets discovered the immense profits to be made in the illegal beer and liquor industry. Before long they controlled whole sections of cities and warred with one another in the streets. Though most gangs are of ethnic origin--Irish, Italian, and Jewish in the main--gangsters of nearly all nationalities are found within the ranks.

Aside from illegal liquor, organized crime deals in prostitution, protection, narcotics, gambling, and many other forms of corruption.

Gangsters keep plush offices in desirable downtown locations. Although some prefer to keep a low profile, many are flashy individuals desirous of attention and publicity. Sharp dressers, they are often charming in public, though dangerous in private.

Hit Man

Gangster Al Capone (1899-1947)

Born Alphonse Capone in Naples, Italy, Al Capone came to New York City with his family as a youngster, and only later moved to Chicago. The results of a youthful knife fight earned him the nickname Scarface. Capone and his Chicago gang eventually came to control most of the illegal bootlegging, prostitution, and gambling operations in that city. Capone's gang brutally murdered many rival gang leaders, eventually committing the infamous St. Valentine's Day Massacre of 1929, in which seven men were machine-gunned to death. He avoided conviction for any of these crimes through the fear instilled by his gang. Finally convicted of federal tax evasion in 1931, he spent eight years in prison. Upon release, Capone retired to Miami, where he later dies.

A gangster character could be the boss of a whole city, part of a city, or merely an underling gangster that works for the boss. Underlings usually have specific areas of responsibility such as overseeing liquor shipments, collecting protection money, etc.

EARNINGS: Middle class to Wealthy.

CONTACTS AND CONNECTIONS: Organized crime, street scene, police, city government, politicians, judges, D.A.s, unions, etc., as well as the local ethnic community and possibly the local church. Your loyal underlings protect you from connection to actual crimes and are willing to go to prison for you.

SKILLS: Bargain, Club, Conceal, Drive Auto, Firearms, Fist/Punch, Grapple, Head Butt, Kick, Knife, Persuade, Psychology.

SPECIAL: -6 to EDU. Most gangsters are immune to sanity losses resulting from witnessing a murder, viewing a corpse, or seeing violence perpetrated against a human being. All gangsters subtract 10+1D6 points from their beginning sanity--a result of the sort of lives they've led. Gangsters also harbor a secret phobia to be chosen by the keeper and exposed when the investigator least expects it. American-born Italian gangsters begin with 1D20+20 points in Italian.

Hit Man

Hit men are the cold-blooded killers of the underworld. Usually hired from somewhere out of town, they arrive, do their work, then quickly disappear. Sociopaths, they seem to lack the ability to empathize with other human beings. Despite this, many marry, raise children, and in all other ways behave like model citizens.

EARNINGS: Upper Lower to Upper Middle class.

CONTACTS AND CONNECTIONS: Few, mostly underworld; people prefer not to know them too well.

SKILLS: Bargain, Clubs, Conceal, Firearms, Fist/Punch, Grapple, Head Butt, Kick, Knife, Sneak, Hide.

SPECIAL: -6 to EDU. Immune to sanity losses resulting from violence committed against human beings. Hit men begin with a penalty of 20+1D6 points subtracted from their current sanity and harbor 1D2 secret phobias.

Shifty Accountant/Lawyer

Organized crime needs its lawyers, accountants, and other business personnel. Due to the nature of their work they are usually kept segregated from the actual crimes, pretending not to know what their employers are really up to. Nevertheless, most are recognized underworld figures well known to the police, the press, and the public as well.

EARNINGS: Middle to Upper Middle class.

CONTACTS AND CONNECTIONS: Organized crime, finance, D.A.s and judges.

SKILLS: Accounting, Bargain, Credit Rating, English, Fast Talk, Law, Persuade, Psychology.

SPECIAL: Due to your position, you can usually lay your hands on large amounts of money--although skimming is a risky business.

Bootlegger/Thug

The soldiers of organized crime. Tough, mean, and loyal, they transfer beer shipments, intimidate enemies, collect debts, and hijack rival gangster's trucks. Arrested, they are expected to take the fall for the gangsters above them. They usually serve only short jail sentences, the mob supporting their families in exchange for their silence and loyalty. Once released they are back in the gang's 'family,' and often in line for possible promotion.

Free lance thugs work as muggers, stick-up men, and armed robbers.

EARNINGS: Upper Lower to Middle class.

CONTACTS AND CONNECTIONS: Organized crime, street scene, local cops, the local ethnic community.

SKILLS: Club, Conceal, Drive Auto/Truck, Firearms, Fist/Punch, Grapple, Head Butt, Kick, Knife.

SPECIAL: -6 to EDU. Sanity losses resulting from witnessing violence against humans are reduced to half the rolled loss. Thugs begin with a penalty of 10+1D6 subtracted from their beginning sanity. They also suffer from a secret phobia.

Bank Robbers Bonnie Parker and Clyde Barrow (1911-1934, 1909-1934)

Bonnie and Clyde are infamous even among their fellow thieves. Their reputation for needless bloodshed and murder, and their tendency to abandon wounded or surrounded gang members make them among the most hated and feared of the depression era bank robbers. Clyde Barrow was born to a poor family in rural Texas. His older brother Buck was a thief as well, and led Clyde into a life of crime while he was still in his teens. Clyde already had a reputation as a robber when he met the thrill-seeking Bonnie Parker in 1930. But shortly afterward Clyde was caught and jailed for almost two years.

When paroled in 1932, Bonnie joined him and the pair committed a string of robberies through Texas, Oklahoma, Missouri, and New Mexico. They preferred small pickings: gas stations, restaurants, and small town banks and businesses--their most lucrative robbery yielding only $1500. Despite their small-time targets, Bonnie and Clyde seemed enamored of senseless violence. Clyde once killed a sheriff and a deputy at a dance, and Bonnie shot a traffic cop for no particular reason. These were needless crimes, indicative of the carefree way they and their gang lived.

Clyde's brother Buck and his wife joined their gang for a while, as did other minor thugs. They lived on the road, camping out in the wilderness or forcing themselves on farm families. In 1933 Clyde abandoned Buck and his wife in Louisiana when a posse surprised them. The following year Bonnie and Clyde were betrayed by an accomplice and gunned down in a shootout with police near Gibsland, Louisiana.

Loan Shark

A loan shark makes a specialty of lending money at exorbitant interest rates. Loan sharks usually have thugs working for them to collect overdue payments and extract vengeance on bad debtors.

EARNINGS: Middle to Upper class.

CONTACTS AND CONNECTIONS: Organized crime, gamblers, police, any debtor owing him a favor.

SKILLS: Accounting, Bargain, Credit Rating, Fast Talk, Persuade, Psychology.

SPECIAL: -2 to EDU.

Bookie

An illegal occupation involving the handling of bets placed on sporting events, political elections and, in particular, horse racing. A bookie often keeps a restaurant or other legitimate business up front, operating multiple phone lines and a tote board in the back.

EARNINGS: Middle to Upper class.

CONTACTS AND CONNECTIONS: Organized crime, gamblers, local police, sports figures.

SKILLS: Accounting, Bargain, Conceal, Credit Rating, Fast Talk, Persuade, Psychology.

SPECIAL: -2 to EDU.

Fence

Fences are the receivers of stolen goods. Paying rates as low as ten cents on a dollar they purchase, store, and resell hot merchandise. Pawn shops are particularly good fronts for fencing operations. Others store their goods in warehouses or even their own homes.

EARNINGS: Lower Middle to Upper Middle class.

CONTACTS AND CONNECTIONS: Street criminals, organized crime, police, your suppliers and customers from the local community.

SKILLS: Accounting, Bargain, Conceal, Credit Rating, Fast Talk, Persuade, Psychology.

SPECIAL: -4 to EDU.

Bank Robber

Bank robbers are independent operators. While the East Coast and to some extent the West Coast are controlled by the urban gangs, these foot-loose criminals are most commonly found in the vast Midwest. Bonnie and Clyde, John Dillinger, Baby-Face Nelson, and Pretty Boy Floyd are only a few of the many. Working in small gangs, bank robbers stay on the move, criss-crossing the country in stolen cars, robbing and murdering, and looting National Guard armories for firearms and ammunition. They sometime have 'Robin Hood' reputations, supposedly burning unregistered mortgages at banks. They rarely commit crimes against the working class, but some have found profit kidnaping businessmen and bankers, then holding them for ransoms.

EARNINGS: Variable.

CONTACTS AND CONNECTIONS: You and the members of your gang probably have an extended network of family and friends scattered across the country. Common folk will often help you out: hiding you in a barn, misdirecting law officers, etc.

SKILLS: Club, Conceal, Drive Auto, Firearms, Fist/Punch, Grapple, Head Butt, Kick, Knives.

SPECIAL: -6 to EDU. Bank robbers are immune to sanity losses resulting from violence committed against humans. However, they begin with a penalty of 10+1D6 subtracted from their sanity points. Each harbors a secret phobia known only to the keeper, as well.

Burglar

Burglars are independent operators though they occasionally employ partners. Cat burglar or otherwise, most prefer to leave little trace of their comings and goings.

EARNINGS: Lower to Lower Middle class.

CONTACTS AND CONNECTIONS: Fences, other burglars. Most keep a low profile.

SKILLS: Conceal, Climb, Hide, Jump, Locksmith, Listen, Sneak, Spot Hidden.

SPECIAL: -4 to EDU. 20 point bonus to Spot Hidden skill.

Pick Pocket

Pick pockets lead desperate, furtive lives. Often they know one another, occasionally teaming up to perform more intricate maneuvers: one making the actual snatch then quickly handing off the prize to the passing partner and relieving himself of any evidence.

EARNINGS: Lower to Upper Lower class.

CONTACTS AND CONNECTIONS: Street scene; also a few cops from previous pinches. Pickpockets often serve as police informants--a dangerous business.

SKILLS: Conceal, Fast Talk, Hide, Listen, Pick Pocket, Sneak, Spot Hidden.

SPECIAL: -4 to EDU.

Hooker

Depending on circumstance, breeding, and background, a prostitute may be an expensive call girl, brothel whore, or street walker.

EARNINGS: Lower to Upper Middle class.

CONTACTS AND CONNECTIONS: Street scene, police, possibly organized crime, personal clientele.

SKILLS: Bargain, Conceal, Fast Talk, Hide, Persuade, Pick Pocket, Psychology.

SPECIAL: +1 to APP, -2 to EDU.

Gambler

Gamblers are the dandies of the criminal world. Sharp dressers, they usually possess some sort of charm, either earthy or sophisticated. Race track touts smoke cigars and wear pork pie hats and loud sport jackets. More sophisticated gamblers frequent the illegal casinos operated by organized crime. Some fly to Cuba for weekends of gambling and legal drinking. A few are known as poker players and are often involved in lengthy, high-stakes games where they may even be backed by outside investors. The lowest frequent alleys and dives, playing craps with loaded dice, or hustling in pool halls.

EARNINGS: Lower to Upper Middle class.

CONTACTS AND CONNECTIONS: Bookies, organized crime, street scene.

SKILLS: Accounting, Bargain, Conceal, Fast Talk, Listen, Persuade, Psychology, Spot Hidden.

SPECIAL: Add +2 to POW for purposes of calculating Luck.

Con Man

Confidence men are smooth talkers. Working alone or in teams, they descend on communities, fleecing citizens of their hard-earned savings. Some schemes are elaborate, involving teams of scam men and rented buildings; others are simple affairs, transactions requiring only one con man and no more than a few minutes.

EARNINGS: Lower to Lower Middle class.

CONTACTS AND CONNECTIONS: Other con men. Denver, Colorado, is the known as a 'safe home' to hundreds of hustlers. Here, con artist Lou Blonger completely controls the police and government and keeps as many as 500 con men under his control, taking a percentage from each one of them.

SKILLS: Bargain, Disguise, Fast Talk, Listen, Persuade, Psychology, Spot Hidden.

SPECIAL: Immune to Fast Talk and Persuade; even Psychology is ineffective unless the user knows the con man well.

Forger/Counterfeiter

The artists of the criminal world, they specialize in forging official deeds and transfers and providing phony signatures. The beginners work manufacturing fake ID for petty criminals; the best engrave plates for counterfeiting U.S. currency.

EARNINGS: Upper Lower to Upper Middle class.

CONTACTS AND CONNECTIONS: Organized crime, street criminals, businessmen.

SKILLS: Accounting, Art, Bargain, Conceal, Spot Hidden, Persuade, Psychology.

SPECIAL: Special skills Drawing, Engraving, knowledge of inks, paper, printing processes, etc.

Punk

The typical young street hood, possibly looking for a chance to hook up with real gangsters. Experience is probably limited to stealing cars, shoplifting, mugging, and burglary.

EARNINGS: Pauper to Lower class.

CONTACTS AND CONNECTIONS: Street criminals, other punks, the local fence, maybe the local gangster; certainly the local police.

SKILLS: Club, Fist/Punch, Grapple, Head Butt, Kick, Knife, Pick Pocket, Throw.

SPECIAL: -6 to EDU.

Spy

Foreign spies in the U.S. were uncommon prior to the War. Since that time, however, more attention has been paid to America. Most spies work for hostile governments but even the friendliest of allies try to keep tabs on one another.

Spies are sometimes foreign ambassadors or embassy workers. Others work under deep cover, posing as members of the community, working a normal job, even marrying and raising families.

EARNINGS: Lower Middle to Upper Middle class.

CONTACTS AND CONNECTIONS: Generally only the person the spy reports to, and any help or connections he may have developed under cover. Specific contacts depend on what the spy's aims are, although they are more than likely involved with the federal government. Spies also know the location of a local safe house or two where investigators on the lam might hide out.

SKILLS: Bargain, Disguise, Fast Talk, Firearms, Hide, Knife, Listen, Other Language, Persuade, Psychology, Sneak, Spot Hidden.

SPECIAL: Although exceptions to the rule might arise, spies are generally immune to Fast Talk, Persuade, and Psychology.

Smuggler

Smuggling is always a lucrative business. During the 1920s most smugglers were involved in the alcohol trade, although some dealt in morphine and other narcotics, and a few in illegal firearms.

Illegal liquor is brought into the country along both the East and West Coasts by large ships anchoring offshore then unloading into small launches. Additional quantities of liquor come in through Canada either crossing the long border in trucks, or shipped over the Great Lakes. High speed launches regularly run liquor across the narrow Detroit River from Windsor to Detroit, counting on their speed to outrun police and Coast Guard vessels constantly on patrol. Cuba is another favorite spot from which both planes and boats are launched toward Florida.

EARNINGS: Lower Middle to Upper Middle class.

CONTACTS AND CONNECTIONS: Organized crime, Coast Guard, U.S. Customs officials.

SKILLS: Accounting, Bargain, Conceal, Fast Talk, Firearms, Listen, Navigate, Other Language, Persuade, Pilot Aircraft, Pilot Boat, Psychology, Spot Hidden.

Journalism

JOURNALISM REACHES NEW heights in the 1920s. Spurred on by such figures as William Randolph Hearst, popular journalism now includes newspapers, magazines, film, and radio. Huge syndicates own chains of papers across the country, supplemented by national magazines and investments in other media.

By nature and profession curious, investigators with journalistic occupations often come into contact with elder secrets while tracking down a story. Murders, cult raids, and strange phenomena all attract a journalist's attention.

Editor

Editors work in the office, assigning reporters stories, writing editorials, dealing with crises, and meeting deadlines. Occasionally they edit. Large newspapers have many editors, including managing editors more involved with business than news. Other editors specialize in business, sports, or some other area.

Small newspapers may have only a single editor who, in fact, may also be the owner as well as the only full-time employee.

Editor Melville Elijah Stone (1848-1929)

Melville Stone founded the *Chicago Daily News* in 1876, and was general manager of the Associated Press from 1893-1921. Born in Illinois, Stone's first newspaper assignment was with the *Chicago Tribune* in 1875. In 1881 he and a partner bought the *Chicago Morning News*, which he renamed the *Chicago Record*. Stone left the U.S. to spend time in Europe, and when he returned in 1891 he organized the Globe National Bank, of which he was president for seven years. Later, while manager of the Associated Press, he helped smooth out treaty negotiations which led to the end of the Russo-Japanese War in 1905. His autobiography, *Fifty Years a Journalist*, was published in 1921.

EARNINGS: Lower Middle to Upper Middle class.

CONTACTS AND CONNECTIONS: The news industry, local government, others.

SKILLS: Accounting, Bargain, Credit Rating, English, Fast Talk, Persuade, Psychology.

Reporter

Reporters work mostly outside the office, gathering stories. Some are assigned to specific beats like the police station or the sports scene. Others cover social events and garden club meetings. The most experienced are made investigative reporters who track down their own stories. These latter are often responsible for exposing government corruption, organized crime, or other malfeasance.

Reporters carry 'press passes' but these are of little value other than to identify an individual as employed by the newspaper. The real work is similar to that of a private detective and reporters usually have to resort to subterfuge to gain the information they really want.

Photojournalist

EARNINGS: Upper Lower to Middle class.

CONTACTS AND CONNECTIONS: Aside from the news industry, many possibilities exist: government and politics, finance, manufacturing, the sports industry, the police department, organized crime, the street scene, and high society, to name a few. Most reporters settle in a particular area where they are most effective. Few, if any, develop all these possible connections.

SKILLS: Bargain, Climb, Conceal, Disguise, English, Fast Talk, Hide, Jump, Listen, Persuade, Psychology, Sneak, Spot Hidden.

SPECIAL: Depending upon the beat the reporter covers, he may have grown calloused to the sight of violence and suffering and may suffer reduced or negated sanity losses for witnessing such things. Keepers will have to judge individual circumstances.

Correspondent Richard Harding Davis (1864-1916)

Davis was an adventurous war correspondent for the *New York Herald* and the *London Times*. He was born in Philadelphia, the son of novelist Rebecca Harding Davis and Philadelphia newspaperman L. Clark Davis. Richard Harding Davis covered the revolution in Cuba in 1895, and the Spanish-American, Greco-Turkish, Boer, and Russo-Japanese Wars, in addition to the first World War. In times of peace he traveled the world writing magazine articles about his journeys. He also wrote a number of short stories, plays, and novels. His style of writing and reporting was dramatic and sensational, occasionally to the point of exaggeration of the facts.

Columnist

Columnists are the celebrities of the newspaper world, well known to their readers. Usually ex-reporters, they work in the office, or at home, usually writing one column per day, five or six days a week. Some are sports columnists, others write for business and finance, society or the entertainment industry. There are columns giving advice to the love-lorn and even astrology columns. The most sophisticated and popular columnists are syndicated to newspapers around the country.

EARNINGS: Lower Middle to Upper Middle class.

CONTACTS AND CONNECTIONS: News industry, others depending on the type of column written.

Columnist Walter Winchell (1897-1972)

Winchell worked his way up from playing vaudeville to become a popular newspaper columnist and radio and television commentator. He was born in New York City and attended public schools before hitting vaudeville. In 1920 he started writing articles for *The Vaudeville News*, and later moved on to writing articles and columns for other papers.

Winchell's gossip columns were the first of their type to become staples in daily newspapers. His often scandalous gossiping made him many enemies in political and entertainment circles but the public clamored for this "dirt." Other writers imitated his column, which gained national circulation in 1929 through the *New York Daily Mirror*. Winchell's writing made use of a number of unique words he himself coined, such as "middle-aisled" for married.

SKILLS: Bargain, Credit Rating, English, Fast Talk, Persuade, Psychology.

Copywriter

Newspapers employ copywriters to turn slap-dash reporting into readable prose. Some are given additional responsibilities carrying with them titles like "Religion Editor."

EARNINGS: Upper Lower to Middle class.

CONTACTS AND CONNECTIONS: Local news industry, reporters and editors in particular.

SKILLS: English, Fast Talk, Listen, Persuade, Psychology.

Foreign Correspondent

Foreign correspondents are the elite of reporters. They work on salary, enjoy expense accounts, and travel the globe. The work is often exciting and sometimes hazardous.

EARNINGS: Lower Middle to Upper Middle class.

CONTACTS AND CONNECTIONS: The worldwide news industry, foreign governments, military, possibly others.

SKILLS: Bargain, Conceal, Fast Talk, Hide, Other Language, Persuade, Psychology, Sneak.

SPECIAL: Veteran journalists who have covered violent events may avoid sanity losses due to human death or maiming. War correspondents enjoy similar immunity. Keepers must judge the circumstances.

Photojournalist

These are reporters that use cameras. A true photojournalist is expected to write prose to accompany his photo articles.

Newsreels come into being in the 1920s. Heavy, bulky 35mm film equipment is hauled around the globe in search of exciting news stories, sporting events, and bathing beauty pageants. Thrills and danger are the key word in the newsreel industry.

Newsreel teams usually number three, one of them an actual reporter who writes the copy while the other two handle the camera, lights, etc. Voice-overs are done at the home studio, based on the written copy.

EARNINGS: Lower Middle to Middle class.

CONTACTS AND CONNECTIONS: The news industry, possibly film and camera manufacturers.

SKILLS: Climb, Bargain, English, Fast Talk, Jump, Other Language, Persuade, Photography, Psychology.

Radio Announcer

The radio industry booms in the 1920s as this magical new medium captures the nation's imagination. The radio announcer/celebrity is just coming into his own.

EARNINGS: Middle to Upper class.

CONTACTS AND CONNECTIONS: The radio and news industry, possibly Hollywood, others depending upon the content of the radio show.

SKILLS: Bargain, Credit Rating, English, Fast Talk, Persuade, Psychology.

Labor, Rural

THIS INCLUDES ALL forms of labor which, for the most part, are conducted away from cities and outdoors. Some are unionized, many are not. Due to the circumstances of the work, many include along with paid wages, room and board as well.

Farmer/Farm Hand

The 1920s are the first decade where the urban population of the U.S. outnumbers the rural population. Independent farmers are finding themselves squeezed between competition from corporate controlled farms and fluctuating commodities markets.

EARNINGS: Upper Lower to Lower Middle class.

CONTACTS AND CONNECTIONS: Local bank, local politicians, state agricultural department.

SKILLS: Accounting, Axe, Bargain, Climb, Credit Rating, Drive Auto/Tractor, Electrical Repair, First Aid, Jump, Mechanical Repair, Medicine (veterinary), Natural History, Operate Heavy Machinery.

SPECIAL: +1 to CON and +1 to STR. Add 20 points to Credit Rating if you own your farm.

Farmer

EARNINGS: Lower to Lower Middle class.

CONTACTS AND CONNECTIONS: Local bank, local politicians, state agricultural department.

SKILLS: Accounting, Bargain, Credit Rating, Drive Auto, Firearms, First Aid, Jump, Medicine (veterinary), Natural History, Ride, Rope.

SPECIAL: +1 to STR and CON. Add 20 points to Credit Rating if you own your own spread.

Ranch Hand/Cowboy

Cowboys still work the ranges and ranches of the west. Some own their own ranches, but many simply hire on where and when work is available. A few have found employment in Hollywood working as stuntmen and extras in the ever-popular westerns. Wyatt Earp currently works as a technical advisor to the film industry.

Lumberjack

Lumberjacks are most often employed by large lumber companies working in the northern U.S. and northwest Canada. Many are of French-Canadian descent.

EARNINGS: Upper Lower class.

CONTACTS AND CONNECTIONS: Few.

SKILLS: Axe, Bargain, Block, Climb, Fist/Punch, Grapple, Head Butt, Kick, Jump.

SPECIAL: +1 to STR and +1 to CON. -2 to EDU. Possibly a bonus of 20 points to French.

Miner

A grueling job most likely in the coal mines of West Virginia, Pennsylvania, and surrounding area. Unions struggle against the mine owners and violence--including bombings and assassinations--is not uncommon.

EARNINGS: Upper Lower class.

CONTACTS AND CONNECTIONS: Union officials and activists.

SKILLS: Climb, Geology, Jump, Operate Heavy Machinery, Spot Hidden.

SPECIAL: +1 to STR, -1 to CON, -2 to EDU. Special dark-acclimated vision adds 20 points to Spot Hidden in the dark. Miners are generally immune to claustrophobia and have a faster than normal crawling speed. Special skills include some knowledge of mine engineering, rigging ropes and braces, and digging and tunneling equipment.

Labor, Urban

DESPITE THE OPPOSITION of big business, the labor movement continues to gain ground throughout the decade. Despised by some, unions are charged with harboring communists and anarchists.

Union Activist

Activists are organizers, leaders, and visionaries--and sometimes malcontents with an axe to grind. In these turbulent times union officials find themselves caught between big business wishing to destroy them, politicians alternately befriending and condemning them, communists and socialists trying to infiltrate their ranks, and criminal mobs trying to take them over.

EARNINGS: Usually out of work.

CONTACTS AND CONNECTIONS: Other labor leaders and activists, possibly socialists, communists, and/or subversives, possibly organized crime.

SKILLS: Accounting, Bargain, Club, Conceal, English, Fast Talk, Fist/Punch, Grapple, Head Butt, Kick, Law, Operate Heavy Machinery, Persuade, Psychology.

Skilled Trade/Mechanic

This occupation includes all types of trades requiring specialized training, time on the job, etc. Carpenters, stone masons, plumbers, electricians, millwrights, mechanics, and others all qualify as skilled trades. They have their own unions--almost guilds--that bargain with contractors, corporate employers, etc.

EARNINGS: Lower Middle class.

CONTACTS AND CONNECTIONS: The union.

SKILLS: Art (carpentry, plumbing, etc.) Climb, Electrical Repair, Mechanical Repair, Operate Heavy Machinery.

SPECIAL: +1 to either CON or STR.

Laborer

This includes factory workers, mill hands, stevedores, road crews, miners, and any other unskilled labor position. Often these jobs are represented by unions, especially in the larger shops, but many employment areas still resist unionization.

EARNINGS: Upper Lower class.

CONTACTS AND CONNECTIONS: Few, if any.

SKILLS: Operate Heavy Machinery.

SPECIAL: +1 to CON or STR, -2 to EDU.

Bus Driver/Streetcar Conductor

Formerly owned by private companies, by the end of the decade most bus and other public transport lines have been taken over by their respective cities or counties. Workers are fully unionized and there seems at last an end to the crippling urban transit strikes of earlier years.

EARNINGS: Lower Middle class.

CONTACTS AND CONNECTIONS: Few.

SKILLS: Accounting, Drive Auto/Bus, Electrical Repair, Mechanical Repair, Navigate, Persuade, Psychology.

SPECIAL: -2 to EDU.

Bartender

A profession made illegal by the Prohibition Act, many still ply their trade in speakeasies and other secret gin joints.

Laborer

EARNINGS: Upper Lower to Lower Middle class.

CONTACTS AND CONNECTIONS: Customers, possibly organized crime.

SKILLS: Accounting, Club, Fast Talk, Fist/Punch, Persuade, Psychology.

SPECIAL: -2 to EDU.

Union Activist Samuel Gompers (1850-1924)

Samuel Gompers was born in London, and moved to the U.S. when he was thirteen. A year later he was registered as the first member of the Cigar-Makers' International Union, an organization which he later made one of the most successful trade unions. Gompers became the first president of the American Federation of Labor in 1886, a post he would be reelected to every year until his death--with the exception of 1895. Gompers' influence kept the labor unions from allying with established political parties, and instead urged them to bargain with employers. He argued against the labor injunctions which the legal system used to break strikes, and lobbied for provisions to the Clayton Antitrust Act of 1914. He also lobbied to regulate working hours and conditions for women and children. Gompers' influence helped to shape the reformation of the U.S. Department of Labor in 1913.

Cocktail Waitress

Again a technically illegal profession, many job opportunities exist working in the illegal speakeasies owned by the mob.

EARNINGS: Upper Lower to Lower Middle class.

CONTACTS AND CONNECTIONS: Customers, organized crime.

SKILLS: Accounting, Fast Talk, Persuade, Psychology.

SPECIAL: +1 to APP, -2 to EDU.

Taxi Driver

Drivers may work for large or small companies, or possibly own their own cab and medallion. Cab companies are set up so that drivers rent cabs and dispatcher service from the company, technically making the drivers free lance operators. Cab rental rates are figured by the fraction of a mile, or by the fraction of the hour when sitting still. Drivers are often required to buy their own gasoline.

In earlier years intense competition among cab drivers led to violence, shootings, and even to cabs being outfitted with iron rams and armor. Most cities now make a practice of bonding each and every cab, and even limiting the number of medallions the city issues. Taxis are required to be fitted with approved meters, periodically checked by the city's taxi board. Drivers are usually required to obtain a special license that includes a background check by the police detective bureau.

EARNINGS: Lower to Upper Lower class.

CONTACTS AND CONNECTIONS: Street scene, possibly a notable customer now and then.

SKILLS: Accounting, Bargain, Drive Auto, Electrical Repair, Fast Talk, Mechanical Repair, Navigate, Persuade, Psychology.

SPECIAL: -2 to EDU.

Law Enforcement

LAW ENFORCEMENT INCLUDES a diverse assortment of uniformed and plainclothes officers employed by local, state, and federal governments, as well as private detectives and others.

Many law enforcement agents become investigators after making discoveries investigating grisly murders or the activities of strange cults.

Uniformed Police Officer

Uniformed police are employed by cities and towns, by county sheriff's department, and state police forces as well. The job may be on foot, behind the wheel of a patrol car, or even sitting at a desk. Most urban officers, however, walk foot patrol--a beat--either alone or in pairs. Police forces are organized along military lines including ranks of sergeant, lieutenant, captain, and chief, among others.

The pay being what it is, many officers work part time as uniformed security guards, or as plainclothes bodyguards. In either case, they are allowed to wear their uniforms.

EARNINGS: Lower Middle class to Middle class.

CONTACTS AND CONNECTIONS: Law enforcement, local shopkeeps and residents, street scene, possibly organized crime.

SKILLS: Club, Drive Automobile, Firearms, Fist/Punch, Grapple, Kick, Law, Persuade, Track.

SPECIAL: +1 to STR and to SIZ. Add 50 bonus points to any weapon or melee skill. Officers on the street are used to a certain level of violence and murder scenes or the sight of gross injuries are unlikely to result in sanity losses.

Police Officer

SPECIAL: Immune to sanity losses resulting from the sight of normal corpses or injuries. Immune to most Fast Talk and Persuade attempts.

Police Detective

The plainclothes branch of police agencies, detectives examine crime scenes, gather evidence, conduct interviews, and try to solve homicides, major burglaries, and other sorts of felonies. They work the streets, often in close cooperation with uniformed patrolmen. They have their own hierarchy of ranks similar to, but separate from, the uniformed officers

EARNINGS: Lower Middle to Middle class.

CONTACTS AND CONNECTIONS: Law enforcement, street scene, coroner's office, possibly organized crime.

SKILLS: Bargain, Drive Auto, Fast Talk, Forensics, Handgun, Law, Listen, Persuade, Psychology, Spot Hidden, Track.

Forensic Specialist

A rather new occupation, the forensic specialist is usually a detective with a knack for collecting and analyzing fingerprints, blood samples, and other forensic evidence. Because of their preoccupation with this pursuit, they are usually passed over in the course of normal promotions.

EARNINGS: Lower Middle to Middle class.

CONTACTS AND CONNECTIONS: Law enforcement, local labs and chemical supply outlets.

SKILLS: Chemistry, Forensics, Law, Medicine, Pharmacy, Photography, Spot Hidden.

SPECIAL: Immune to sanity losses due to viewing most murder or injury scenes.

Agency Detective

Numerous well-known detective agencies exist: the Pinkerton and Burns agencies to name only two. Large agencies employ two types of agents: security guards and operatives. Guards are uniformed patrolmen, hired by companies and individuals to protect property and people against burglars, assassins, and kidnapers. Use the Uniformed Police Officer's description for these characters. Company Operatives are plainclothes detectives sent out on cases requiring them to solve mysteries, stop murders, etc.

EARNINGS: Lower Middle to Middle class.

CONTACTS AND CONNECTIONS: Local law enforcement, clients.

SKILLS: Bargain, Fast Talk, Fist/Punch, Grapple, Handgun, Hide, Law, Library Use, Persuade, Psychology, Sneak, Track.

SPECIAL: Immunity to sanity losses from corpses, injuries, etc.

Private Eye

The Private Eye is a free-lance detective with his own small agency, possibly employing an assistant and a secretary. Most private eyes have spent time working as operatives with national agencies or city police forces before going out on their own. A special license is required.

EARNINGS: Upper Lower to Lower Middle class.

CONTACTS AND CONNECTIONS: Many law and criminal connections, newspaper morgues, switchboard operators, secretaries.

SKILLS: Accounting, Bargain, Climb, Disguise, Drive Auto, Fast Talk, Fist/Punch, Forensics, Grapple, Head Butt, Hide, Jump, Kick, Law, Library Use, Persuade, Sneak, Swim, Track.

SPECIAL: Lowered or negated sanity losses when viewing murder victims, gross injuries, etc.

Federal Agents

There are a vast variety of federal law enforcement agents. Some are uniformed, such as the U.S. Marshals and some agents of the Customs Department. Use the Uniformed Police Officers descriptions for these characters. Others--the Bureau of Investigation, the Secret Service, etc--are plainclothes and operate similar to detectives.

EARNINGS: Lower Middle to Upper Middle class.

CONTACTS AND CONNECTIONS: Federal contacts, possibly organized crime.

SKILLS: Bargain, Drive Auto, Fast Talk, Firearms, Fist/Punch, Forensics, Grapple, Hide, Law, Persuade, Sneak, Spot Hidden, Track.

SPECIAL: As with other law enforcement occupations, past exposure to death and injury often reduces or eliminates sanity losses.

Detective William John Burns (1861-1932)

Burns was one of the most successful lawmen of the time. As an investigator for the U.S. Attorney General during Teddy Roosevelt's administration, Burns exposed the involvement of several Oregon congressmen in a land fraud scheme. He later served as director of the Department of Justice's Bureau of Investigation, from 1921-1924, prior to J. Edgar Hoover. He also headed the highly respected William J. Burns International Detective Agency.

Federal Agent Elliot Ness (1903-1957)

Elliot Ness was a federal agent in the city of Chicago during the late 1920s and 1930s. Ness and his men gained fame for their dogged pursuit of Chicago gang leader Al Capone. Ness was born in Chicago, and graduated from the University of Chicago. At the age of twenty-six he was made a special agent of the U.S. Department of Justice and assigned to head the prohibition bureau for Chicago. More specifically, his assignment was to topple Capone's criminal organization. For this task Ness assembled a band of eight young agents whom he felt were incorruptible--"The Untouchables." Ness and his men raided speakeasies, breweries, and other examples of Capone's illegal operations. The resultant headlines brought fame to both Ness and Capone, though Ness's inability to gain a conviction against Capone made him a target of ridicule. Capone's luck ran out in 1931, when--with Ness's aid--he was convicted of federal tax evasion. From 1933-1935 Ness led the Alcohol Tax Unit of the U.S. Treasury Department. He then became the Director of Public Safety in Cleveland from 1935-1941, and did more security work for the federal government during the Second World War.

Western Lawman

The Old West still lives in certain parts of the country. Although train robbers and professional gunfighters are mostly a thing of the past, cattle rustlers, armed robbers, and just plain 'bad folk' are still around. The western lawman is probably a county sheriff or deputy responsible for a large area, patrolling in an automobile, truck, or on horseback.

EARNINGS: Upper Lower to Lower Middle class.

CONTACTS AND CONNECTIONS: Local officials, local residents, local criminals.

SKILLS: Drive Auto, Firearms, Fist/Punch, Grapple, Head Butt, Kick, Law, Persuade, Psychology, Ride, Rope, Track.

SPECIAL: Resistant to sanity losses resulting from witnessing murder, human violence, or normal injury. Add 50 bonus points to Firearm skills.

Bounty Hunter

Bounty Hunters are a leftover from an earlier era but still useful tracking down and returning fugitives from justice. Bounty hunters are free lancers most often employed by Bondsmen to track down bail jumpers. Bounty hunters freely cross state lines in pursuit of their quarry and show little regard for civil rights and other technicalities when capturing their prey. Breaking and entering, illegal phone taps, threats, and physical abuse are all part of the successful bounty hunter's bag of tricks. Although a captured fugitive might complain to authorities about his rights being violated, grateful police are slow to follow up on these charges.

EARNINGS: Upper Lower to Lower Middle class.

CONTACTS AND CONNECTIONS: Bail bondsmen, local police.

SKILLS: Accounting, Bargain, Climb, Drive Auto, Electrical Repair, Fast Talk, Firearms, Fist/Punch, Grapple, Head Butt, Hide, Jump, Kick, Law, Persuade, Psychology, Sneak.

SPECIAL: +1 to STR and +1 to SIZ. Although violence and criminals are all part of his work, the bounty hunter is rarely exposed to murder or maiming. In most instances they suffer normal sanity losses.

The Legal Profession

THE LEGAL PROFESSION of the 1920s offered many of the same opportunities it does today. Criminal lawyers specialize in felony cases while civil lawyers handle lawsuits. Tax attorneys are hired by banks and businesses, while others specialize in divorce or other specific area. Few attorneys become investigators unless drawn in by the problems of a client, or possibly while prosecuting a local cult leader for various crimes.

Judge Oliver Wendell Holmes (1841-1935)

Holmes served on the U.S. Supreme Court for nearly 30 years. Born in Boston, his father was a famous writer, physician, and wit. Holmes Jr. served in the Union Army during the Civil War, was wounded three times, and retired with the rank of lieutenant colonel. After the war he enrolled in Harvard law school, and eventually co-edited the *American Law Review*. He wrote *The Common Law* in 1881, and the following year became a professor of Law at Harvard and also won an appointment to the Supreme Judicial Court of Massachusetts. In 1899 he became Chief Justice of Massachusetts, and in 1902 President Teddy Roosevelt made him an associate justice of the U.S. Supreme Court. There Holmes left an enduring mark on the American judicial system.

Holmes' frequent dissenting opinions earned him the epithet "The Great Dissenter." His belief in a legal system tempered to fit the changing social climate of the nation met with early resistance, but was soon accepted--and continues to this day. He also felt that the individual states should have more control over their own legislation and judicial decisions, stances which also brought resistance from others on the high court. Nevertheless, Holmes was popular among the citizenry as a down-to-earth jurist.

Judge

Practicing Attorney

Attorneys are licensed by individual states, most of them requiring an attorney to have a minimum of a high school education, plus either attendance at an accredited law school or two or three years spent working under a licensed attorney. An examination administered by the State Bar Association rates attorneys and awards licenses. An understanding known as 'comity' allows attorneys to practice law in different states regardless of where their license was obtained.

Attorneys can be employed by large law firms, directly by corporations, or simply hang out their shingle and hope to attract a practice.

EARNINGS: Lower Middle to Upper class.

CONTACTS AND CONNECTIONS: Legal connections, possibly criminal connections, depending on clientele.

SKILLS: Accounting, Bargain, Credit Rating, English, Fast Talk, Law, Library Use, Persuade, Psychology.

SPECIAL: Licensed attorneys add 20 points to their Credit Rating.

Prosecuting Attorney

Prosecuting attorneys are employed by local, state, or federal government agencies to prosecute cases brought by the state against individuals. "District Attorney" is only one of many such titles. Smaller communities, rather than keep an attorney on salary, hire local attorneys to handle cases as they arise.

EARNINGS: Lower Middle to Upper Middle class.

CONTACTS AND CONNECTIONS: Legal connections, possibly organized crime.

SKILLS: Bargain, Credit Rating, English, Fast Talk, Law, Library Use, Persuade, Psychology.

SPECIAL: This type of attorney adds 30 points to his Credit Rating.

Judge

Judges are either appointed or elected, sometimes for a term of specified length, other times for life. Judges are always licensed attorneys whether they sit on the smallest bench in a far off Western town, or on the bench of the Federal Supreme Court.

EARNINGS: Middle to Upper class.

CONTACTS AND CONNECTIONS: Legal connections, possibly organized crime.

SKILLS: Bargain, Credit Rating, English, Fast Talk, Law, Library Use, Persuade, Psychology.

SPECIAL: Judges add 40 points to their Credit Rating.

Bail Bondsman

Bail Bondsman operate their own businesses, usually out of offices located very near the county jail or other arrest holding facility. They provide funds that allow those charged with crimes to 'make bail' and go free. Bondsman usually require the person to put up some of their own money in cash--usually 10-20% of the bond--along with substantial real property signed over to the bail bondsman, intended to protect him against loss should the accused person flee while awaiting trial or sentencing. This security is usually real estate, but automobiles or other items of value can sometimes be negotiated. Bail bondsmen employ bounty hunters to track down those who skip bail.

EARNINGS: Middle to Upper class.

CONTACTS AND CONNECTIONS: Police, courts, street scene, organized crime, bounty hunters.

SKILLS: Accounting, Bargain, Credit Rating, Fast Talk, Law, Persuade, Psychology.

Attorney General Harlan F. Stone (1872-1946)

Stone was a noted lawyer, jurist, and Attorney General of the United States. He was born in Chesterfield, New Hampshire, to parents who were farmers. He studied at Amherst College, graduating in 1894 and moving on to study law at Columbia, where he eventually taught the subject from 1899-1905. From 1910 to 1923 Stone was the dean of the Columbia University Law School. He also practiced law in New York City, specializing in corporate law.

In 1924 Stone was appointed attorney general of the United States. As the federal government's chief legal officer, Stone first cleaned up scandals within the very Department of Justice in which he served. He became an associate justice on the U.S. Supreme Court in 1925, and later chief justice from 1941-1946. Though he himself was a conservative, Stone sometimes sided with fellow justice Oliver Wendell Holmes in cases concerned with progressive social ramifications.

The Medical Profession

PEOPLE INVOLVED IN medical occupations are more often enticed into becoming investigators after seeing something strange in an emergency or delivery room. Odd wounds, strange diseases, inexplicable growths, and grotesque stillbirths are all possibilities.

Physicians

Physicians are licensed by individual states, most requiring a minimum of two years attendance at an accredited medical school. These requirements, however, are but a recent development. Many older physicians first obtained their licenses long before such strict regulations were in effect and continue to hold them despite failing to have ever attended medical school.

At the beginning of this century there were over 160 medical schools in the U.S. but no governing agency to oversee them. Many of these schools were inadequate, and some downright frauds. Even the best of them seldom required more than a high school education from its applicants. In 1904 the AMA (American Medical Association) began critically rating these schools and by 1923 their number had fallen to eighty, seventy-four of which required a minimum two years of college before entry.

Younger doctors will have passed through the school and licensing system established in later years. Older physicians have probably practiced since before the days of strict licensing and may or may not be proficient in modern methods. Some survive from the day when a doctor was expected to be a barber, as well.

A doctor can choose to be a General Practitioner with a rural or neighborhood practice in or near a small town or city. In rural areas such small practices can still be purchased from retiring physicians by younger doctors looking to establish themselves. Many physicians are employed by large urban hospitals, allowing them to specialize in things like pathology, toxicology, orthopedics, and even brain surgery. Doctors may also serve as part or full-time Medical Examiners, conducting autopsies and signing death certificates for the city, county, or state.

EARNINGS: Middle to Upper class.

CONTACTS AND CONNECTIONS: High community status; an accredited physician might be able to talk his way past many standard hospital regulations, obtaining evidence not readily available to others.

SKILLS: Accounting, Bargain, Biology, Credit Rating, First Aid, Latin, Library Use, Medicine, Persuade, Pharmacy, Psychoanalysis, Psychology.

SPECIAL: Add 30 points to Credit Rating. Due to the nature of the work, physicians may be immune to some sanity losses caused by injury and death. Medical examiners are particularly resistant to these sorts of losses.

Physician

Nurse

Nurses are trained medical assistants, sometimes male, but far more often female. Nursing schools have been established around the country and most states now require successful completion of an accredited nursing course before awarding a license. Many older nurses, however, have been in the profession since long before there were such things.

EARNINGS: Lower Middle to Middle class.

CONTACTS AND CONNECTIONS: Access to drugs, equipment, medical records.

SKILLS: Biology, Credit Rating, First Aid, Medicine, Persuade, Pharmacy, Psychology.

SPECIAL: Add 10 points to Credit Rating. Nurses share an immunity similar to physicians regarding certain sanity losses.

Dentist

Dentists are licensed by the state in much the same way as physicians. Dentists most often open small offices and develop their own practices.

EARNINGS: Lower Middle to Upper Middle class.

CONTACTS AND CONNECTIONS: Clientele.

SKILLS: Accounting, Bargain, Credit Rating, First Aid, Library Use, Medicine, Persuade, Pharmacy, Psychology.

Physicians William James and Charles Horace Mayo (1861-1939, 1865-1939)

William and Charles were the sons of William Worrall Mayo, one of the leading physicians of his day. The Mayo family practiced medicine in Minnesota, and started the Mayo Clinic in Rochester, Minnesota in 1889 (though it would not be officially named so until 1903).

William Mayo, Jr, the older of the two sons, was famous for his surgical treatments of cancer, gallstones, and intestinal operations. He graduated from the University of Michigan medical school in 1883. William Mayo was an Army Medical Crops volunteer in the World War, and in 1921 was made a brigadier general in the medical reserve.

Charles Mayo's most famous contribution to surgical treatments was a reduction of the hazards associated with goiter surgery. Charles served alongside his brother William during the War and received similar awards. Charles taught surgery at the Mayo Foundation from 1915-1936 and at the University of Minnesota from 1919-1936, and also served as the health officer of Rochester from 1912-1937.

In conjunction with the Mayo Clinic, the Mayos also founded the Mayo Foundation for Medical Education and Research, contributing millions of dollars to the project. The Foundation became one of the most important centers of medical research in the world.

SPECIAL: Add 10 bonus points to Credit Rating. You have ready access to special gases and anesthetics, and the knowledge to use them.

Plastic Surgeon

This is a new field and particularly popular in Hollywood where closeup cameras readily reveal the disastrous effects of aging; face lifts are already common within the film community. Gangsters and other criminals have also taken advantage of this science, seeking to alter their appearance and escape recognition. Plastic surgeons are all licensed physicians specializing in what is commonly known as cosmetic surgery.

EARNINGS: Middle to Upper Middle class.

CONTACTS AND CONNECTIONS: Medical profession, Hollywood, possibly criminal figures.

SKILLS: Accounting, Bargain, Biology, Credit Rating, First Aid, Latin, Library use, Medicine, Pharmacy, Persuade, Psychology.

SPECIAL: Add 20 points to Credit Rating.

Pharmacist

Oddly enough, pharmacists have long been more closely regulated than physicians. They are licensed by individual states, most of them requiring a high school education and three years of pharmacy school. There are currently seventy to eighty pharmacy schools in the U.S. A pharmacist may be employed in a hospital or a drug store, or even seek to own his own store.

EARNINGS: Middle to Upper Middle class.

CONTACTS AND CONNECTIONS: Access to various drugs, possible good standing in the local community, local physicians and hospitals.

SKILLS: Accounting, Bargain, Biology, Credit Rating, English, First Aid, Latin, Library Use, Pharmacy, Persuade, Psychology.

SPECIAL: Add 10 bonus points to Credit Rating.

Technician

Technicians may be trained to work in X-ray rooms, pathology labs, or other specialized areas. Employment as a technician does not strictly require higher education, though employers often ask for education beyond high school.

EARNINGS: Lower Middle to Middle class.

CONTACTS AND CONNECTIONS: Medical and hospital laboratory equipment, drugs, chemicals.

SKILLS: Biology, Chemistry, Electrical Repair, Library Use, Mechanical Repair, Medicine, Pharmacy, Photography.

SPECIAL: Add 10 bonus points to Credit Rating.

Orderly

The typical hospital orderly is in charge of emptying wastes, cleaning rooms, taxiing patients, and any other odd job requiring slightly more skill than a janitor.

EARNINGS: Upper Lower class.

CONTACTS AND CONNECTIONS: Hospital. Access to drugs, medical records, etc.

SKILLS: Electrical Repair, Fast Talk, First Aid, Hide, Mechanical Repair, Sneak.

SPECIAL: -2 to EDU.

Forensic Surgeon

A specialized occupation, most forensic surgeons are employed by a city, county, or state to conduct autopsies, determine causes of death, and make recommendations to the prosecutor's office. Forensic surgeons are often called to give testimony at criminal proceedings.

EARNINGS: Middle to Upper Middle class.

CONTACTS AND CONNECTIONS: Laboratory facilities, law enforcement and the medical profession.

SKILLS: Biology, Credit Rating, First Aid, Forensic Surgery, Library Use, Medicine, Pharmacy.

SPECIAL: Immune to sanity losses caused by gore and/or bad smells. A licensed physician, add 20 points to Credit Rating.

Mental Health

THOSE RESPONSIBLE FOR the treatment and care of the mentally ill often hear or see inexplicable things, eventually leading to the furtive life of an investigator.

Psychiatrists Karl and William Menninger (1893-1990, 1899-1966)

With their father Charles Menninger, Karl and William Menninger founded the Menninger Clinic and the Menninger Foundation in 1919 in Topeka, Kansas. These organizations were administered and financed largely by the Menninger family. The brothers were born and kept their practices in Topeka.

Karl Menninger graduated from the University of Wisconsin and got his M.D. from Harvard. He sought to improve psychiatric care facilities and stressed more personalized treatments of mental patients. A Freudian, Karl Menninger's books included *The Human Mind* (1930), which strongly influenced public attitudes toward the treatment of mental disorders.

William Menninger attended college in Topeka and received his M.D. from Cornell. William served as chief psychiatric consultant to the Surgeon General of the U.S. Army during World War II, for which he won a Distinguished Service Medal. After the war he wrote such books as *Psychiatry in a Troubled World* and *Psychiatry: Its Evolution and Present Status* (both 1948). He was also a leader of the Boy Scout movement.

Alienist

Psychiatry is not a recognized treatment in the U.S. There are no licensing requirements and practicing alienists run the risk of being charged with malpractice. It is safest for the psychiatrist to call himself a "psychologist," taking patients on referral from other physicians. Many alienists are physicians themselves, attracted to the therapy because of the emotional disorders of some of their patients. Eventually recognized by the AMA and the federal government, practicing psychiatrists will eventually be licensed as such, but will be required to have first obtained a medical degree.

Those wishing to have made a serious study of psychotherapeutic methods will have probably had to spend some time in Europe working in an appropriate clinic or with a private practitioner.

EARNINGS: Lower Middle to Middle class.

Madhouse Attendant

CONTACTS AND CONNECTIONS: Others in the psychological field. May have personally met Sigmund Freud, Carl Jung, or other prominent European psychologist.

SKILLS: Accounting, Bargain, Biology, Fast Talk, Hypnotism, Library Use, Medicine, Other Language, Persuade, Pharmacy, Psychoanalysis, Psychology.

SPECIAL: A trained psychoanalyst can use his techniques to negate the effects of his own temporary insanity. Successful ne-

Psychologist Alfred Adler (1870-1937)

Adler was a noted Austrian psychologist who worked with Sigmund Freud from 1902-1911. Adler specialized in child psychology and development, and in studies of the inferiority complex. He theorized that the individual is capable of overcoming his own psychological problems, provided he is first aware of such defects. Adler became the director of the first child psychology clinic in 1920, in Vienna. Like his friend Freud, Adler left Austria when the Nazis came to power, relocating to New York City in 1934.

gation requires a Psychoanalysis roll. Regardless of the outcome, the sanity point losses apply.

Psychologist

A rather new field involving the study of human behavior. Many psychologists are professors and researchers but industry is currently showing interest in the possibility of increasing productivity through improved working conditions.

EARNINGS: Lower Middle to Middle class.

CONTACTS AND CONNECTIONS: The psychological community.

SKILLS: Account, Bargain, Library Use, Persuade, Psychoanalysis, Psychology.

Madhouse Attendant

Although there are private sanitariums for those few that can afford them, the vast bulk of the mentally ill are housed in state and county facilities. Aside from a few doctors and nurses, they employ a large number of attendants, often chosen for their strength and size.

EARNINGS: Upper Lower class.

CONTACTS AND CONNECTIONS: Access to medical records as well as drugs and other medical supplies.

SKILLS: Club, Fast Talk, First Aid, Fist/Punch, Grapple, Head Butt, Kick, Listen, Persuade, Psychology, Sneak.

SPECIAL: +1 to STR and +1 to SIZ. -2 to EDU.

Mental Health Reformer Clifford Beers (1876-1943)

Beers, a Yale graduate, was the founder of the mental health care movement in the United States. His brother died of epilepsy in 1900, and Beers himself developed a severe mental illness. Moving through a variety of institutions and often savage treatments, Beers gradually came to his senses and thereafter set out to reform the treatment of mental patients. He wrote of his experiences in *A Mind That Found Itself* (1908), and a year later helped found the National Committee for Mental Hygiene. Beers also founded the American Foundation for Mental Hygiene, a research institute, in 1928. He led the first International Congress on Mental Hygiene

Military

THE U.S. MILITARY consists of two major branches: the Army and the Navy. Under the command of the Navy are the U.S. Marines and, in time of war, the U.S. Coast Guard as well. A separate Air Force lies in the future but for now all air power is in the hands of the Army and Navy. The Army consists of infantry, artillery, and tank forces, as well as its air branch. The Navy patrols the oceans with an array of battleships, cruisers, and destroyers, as well as a number of aircraft carriers and a fleet of submarines. The Marines, under command of the Navy Department, are similar to the Army but specialize in beach assaults and other tactics. The Coast Guard, in peacetime, is charged with keeping the shores patrolled, capturing smugglers, and conducting maritime rescue operations.

There is of yet no CIA and intelligence gathering for the U.S. is presently handled by Army Intelligence, and Navy Intelligence.

Women are represented in all branches of the military but in strictly non-combatant rolls.

Military Officer

Officers are command rank and most commissions demand some sort of higher education. The armed services have established officer training programs (ROTC) at most major universities and, with his tuition paid by the military, a cadet simultaneously trains for the military while attending school. Upon graduation he is promoted to the

Sergeant Alvin York (1887-1964)

York was an American soldier who fought heroically in France during the War. York was a simple, gentle man, born in the mountains of Tennessee, where he became a crack marksman. York was deeply religious and pacifistic, and balked at entering the service, but his local priest urged him to do his duty for his country. He is famous for singlehandedly killing twenty German soldiers and--by forcing a German officer to order his men to surrender--capturing another 130 men and over thirty machine guns. For this act of bravery York was awarded the U.S. Medal of Honor and the French Croix de Guerre. After the war, York set up a foundation for the education of mountain children and also spoke out in support of prohibition and world peace. His story was filmed as *Sergeant York* in 1941 with Gary Cooper in the title role. At the time of the incident cited above, however, York was only a corporal.

rank of Army or Marine Second Lieutenant, or Naval Ensign, and assigned to a station. Usually they owe the government four years active service after which time they may return to civilian life. Many of the officers trained this way hold professional commissions and serve as doctors, lawyers, or engineers.

Those looking for a life's career in the military try to get themselves appointed to one of the military academies: the Army's West Point, or the Navy's Annapolis. Its hard to beat the respect an officer gains having graduating from one of these schools. Once out of school some officers opt for special training such as air pilot or other.

Occasionally an experienced and exceptionally worthy enlisted man is promoted to 'Warrant Officer.' Although technically at the bottom of the officers' list of ranks, the time and experience required to achieve this promotion carry a respect and reverence far exceeding that of any junior or middle-grade officer.

Most commissions are for life. Even a long-retired officer has the right to call himself "Captain," "General," or whatever.

EARNINGS: Upper Lower to Upper Middle class.

CONTACTS AND CONNECTIONS: Military, federal government.

SKILLS: Bargain, Credit Rating, Dodge, Fast Talk, Fist/Punch, Grapple, Handgun, Head Butt, Hide, Jump, Kick, Navigate, Persuade, Psychology, Sneak.

SPECIAL: Add +1 to EDU, 10 points to Credit Rating. Veterans of the World War are immune to sanity losses stemming from dead bodies, gross injuries, etc. However, such characters suffer from a secret phobia.

Soldier/Marine

This refers to the enlisted ranks of the Army and Marines and include the lowest ranks of private up through Master or Gunnery Sergeant. Although technically outranked by

Soldier

even the freshest of second lieutenants, veteran sergeants are respected by even the highest-ranking officers. Standard enlistment is for six years including four years active duty, and two in standby (inactive) reserve.

All enlisted men receive basic training--'boot camp'--where raw recruits are taught how to march, shoot, and salute. Upon graduation from basic training, most are assigned to the infantry, although the army also needs men for artillery and tank corps as well as the ever-growing Army Air Force. A few are trained for non-combat roles such as air controller, mechanic, clerk, or even officer's steward. Marines, while technically part of the Navy, are similar to soldiers in background, training, and skills.

EARNINGS: Upper Lower to Middle class.

CONTACTS AND CONNECTIONS: Military, Veteran's Administration.

SKILLS: Bayonet, Fist/Punch, Grapple, Head Butt, Kick, Knife, Rifle, Throw, plus possible specialties such as Artillery, Drive Tank, Electrical Repair, Mechanical Repair, Medicine (hospital corpsman), etc.

SPECIAL: -2 to EDU. Add 50 bonus points to any combat or firearm skills. Soldier and Marine war veterans are immune to some sanity losses, but suffer from a secret phobia. Upon death they are entitled to a free head stone courtesy of the U.S. government.

Flying Ace Eddie Rickenbacker (1890-1973)

In the War Eddie Rickenbacker shot down twenty-two planes and four balloons, thus becoming America's leading air ace. Rickenbacker was born in Columbus, Ohio, and left school at the age of twelve to support his family after his father died. He completed his education by taking correspondence courses, and eventually became an auto mechanic and an internationally known race car driver. In 1917 he enlisted in the army, where he initially worked as a driver and engineering officer before becoming a pilot. After the war Rickenbacker worked for various automobile manufacturers and became the owner of the Indianapolis Speedway. In 1938 he also became president of Eastern Airlines, a post which he held for over twenty years.

Sailor

Sailors are trained in either the Navy or the Coast Guard. Like their counterparts in the Army, all sailors go through an initial period of basic training. Upon graduation they are assigned rates and stations. Although many sailors serve in the traditional roles of Boatswain's Mate or Fireman rating (ship's engine man) the Navy also has a need for technically trained mechanics, radio operators, air controllers, etc. The highest enlisted rank is Chief Petty Officer which carries with it a prestige respected by even high-ranking officers.

Enlistments are for six years, usually four years of active duty followed by two years of inactive reserve commitment during which the sailor can be called to serve in times of national emergency.

EARNINGS: Upper Lower to Middle class.

CONTACTS AND CONNECTIONS: Military, Veterans' Admin.

SKILLS: Climb, Fist/Punch, Grapple, Handgun, Head Butt, Jump, Kick, Navigate, Rifle, Swim. Possibly specialties such as Accounting, Artillery, Mechanical Repair, Operate Heavy Machinery, etc.

SPECIAL: -2 to EDU. Sailors saw less action than other servicemen. Only those that can 'verify' exposure to the agonies of war can claim immunity to sanity losses like other veterans.

Mercenary

Military mercenaries are professional soldiers hiring themselves out to fight small wars, stage revolutions, or quell rebellions. Most have legitimate military experience, probably in the Great War, but perhaps in something more exotic like the French Foreign Legion.

EARNINGS: Lower Middle to Middle class.

CONTACTS AND CONNECTIONS: Mercenary networks, illegal arms dealers, small governments, multi-national corporations.

SKILLS: Bargain, Bayonet, Climb, Club, Firearms, Fist/Punch, Garrotte, Grapple, Head Butt, Hide, Jump, Kick, Knife, Navigate, Track, Sneak, Swim.

SPECIAL: Add 100 bonus points to any combat or weapons skills.

Politics

POLITICS EMPLOY A good many people in America. Elections take place regularly and campaigning by officials is nearly a full-time affair. As busy as they are, few have the opportunity to notice the oddities in life and they will most likely have to be dragged into a mystery before becoming investigators.

Elected Official

Popularly elected officials enjoy prestige commensurate with their position. Small town mayors and township supervisors find their influence extends little beyond their municipality's borders. Often these jobs are only part-time, paying but small compensation. The mayors of big cities are well-paid, however, often ruling their cities like little kingdoms and wielding more influence and power than the governor of their respective state.

Mayor James Curley (1874-1958)

Born in Boston, Curley served as a Democratic state legislator, a member of the U.S. House of Representatives, and as governor of Massachusetts. He also served as Mayor of Boston from 1914-1918, 1922-1926, 1930-1934, and 1946-1950. Curley was constantly under investigation for various charges of corruption. He was found guilty of fraud in 1938 and fined $30,000--but the citizens of Boston donated money to pay the fine. Nevertheless he was reelected several times, and was popular with the poorer citizens of Boston. Curley was convicted of mail fraud in 1947 and sent to prison, but President Harry Truman gave him a full pardon in 1950.

Elected Official

Socialist Eugene V. Debs (1855-1926)

Debs is an important leader in the American labor movement. He was born in Indiana and began working on the railroad at the age of fifteen. He became a locomotive fireman and eventually served as the national secretary and treasurer of the Brotherhood of Locomotive Firemen from 1880-1893. He was also in the Indiana state legislature from 1885-1892. He started the American Railway Union in 1893. In support of a strike by workers at the Pullman manufacturing plant, the ARU members refused to pull any Pullman cars. President Grover Cleveland sent federal troops to break up the strike and Debs was imprisoned. While in prison he became a socialist, and ran for the U.S. presidency as a Socialist in 1904, 1908, 1912, and 1920. After making a speech condemning the war in 1918, Debs was imprisoned under the Espionage Act and sentenced to ten years. Nevertheless he again ran for the presidency in 1920, garnering nearly a million votes. While in prison he wrote *Walls and Bars*, a book about prison conditions. In 1921 Debs' sentence was commuted by President Warren G. Harding.

Local Representatives and Senators elected to state houses enjoy a fair amount of respect, particularly with the business community, and often at a statewide level. Governors, of course, are responsible for entire states and have connections across the country.

Suffrage Leader Carrie Chapman Catt (1859-1947)

Catt was a campaigner for international women's suffrage. She was born in Wisconsin, and attended Iowa State College. She became a schoolteacher, and later the first woman superintendent of schools in Mason City, Iowa. Carrie Chapman Catt began her crusade for women's suffrage in 1887, and gave many lectures on the subject. She was president of the National American Woman Suffrage Association from 1900-1904 and 1915-1920, and president of the International Woman Suffrage Alliance 1904-1923. Catt founded the National League of Women Voters in 1919 to teach women about public affairs so that they could vote responsibly. In 1920 the 19th Amendment to the Constitution grants women the right to vote. Carrie Chapman Catt also founded the National Committee on the Cause and Cure of War in 1925, an organization which later became the Women's Action Committee for Victory and a Lasting Peace.

Federal positions carry the most clout. States send a number of Representatives to Congress based upon population count and the House seats over 400 members, each elected to a two-year term. Each state, regardless of size, also sends two Senators to Washington. Elected to six-year terms and numbering less than a hundred, senators hold considerably more influence than Representatives and some elder senators receive nearly as much respect as the president.

EARNINGS: Middle to Upper class.

CONTACTS AND CONNECTIONS: Government, news media, big business, foreign governments, possibly organized crime.

SKILLS: Bargain, Credit Rating, English, Fast Talk, Persuade, Psychology.

SPECIAL: Add +1 to APP. Add a bonus to Credit Rating between 5 points (small town mayor) and 50 points (senior senator), depending upon the office.

Governor Huey Long (1893-1935)

Huey Long held posts as governor and senator from Louisiana. Long was born in Winnfield, Louisiana, and studied law at the University of Oklahoma and at Tulane. He was first elected governor in 1928, and set about instituting reforms that promised to "share the wealth" so that everyone would prosper. His involvement in nearly every level of Louisiana politics earned him the nickname "the Kingfish," and two unsuccessful attempts to impeach him. His near-dictatorial rule of the state brought about public works and social welfare programs that greatly improved Louisiana. In 1930 Long ran for the U.S. Senate while still governor. Winning the election, he refused to give up his governorship until one of his friends could take office in 1932. While many approved of the Kingfish's brand of politics, he had many opponents. His clashes with President Franklin Delano Roosevelt nearly split the Democratic Party. In 1935 Long was assassinated at the Louisiana state capitol building in Baton Rouge. Several members of Huey Long's administration were convicted of fraud in 1939. Earl Long, Huey's younger brother and a political enemy, took over the governorship in that year after Governor Leche resigned amidst the scandal.

Ambassador

Ambassadors are appointed to their positions, often as a reward for services rendered during the campaign. Despite this, efforts are made to send qualified ambassadors to the more important nations, reserving the smaller countries for political rewards.

EARNINGS: Upper class.

CONTACTS AND CONNECTIONS: Federal government, news media, foreign governments.

SKILLS: Bargain, Credit Rating, English, Fast Talk, Other Language, Persuade.

SPECIAL: +1 to APP. Bonus 30 points to Credit Rating.

Political Boss

Bosses never run for office and, in fact, shun the limelight. These are the men who gather in smoke-filled back rooms to wheel and deal, to make and break candidates.

EARNINGS: Upper Middle to Wealthy.

CONTACTS AND CONNECTIONS: News media, finance, big business, organized crime.

SKILLS: Accounting, Bargain, Credit Rating, Fast Talk, Persuade, Psychology.

SPECIAL: 20 point bonus to Credit Rating.

Communist/Radical

The other side of the political coin, radicals work in the streets selling newspapers, organizing rallies, and talking to the public. Others, less respectful of the law, infiltrate unions, incite riots, or even engage in terrorist bombings.

EARNINGS: Generally a non-profit enterprise.

CONTACTS AND CONNECTIONS: Other radicals, artists and writers, unions.

SKILLS: Club, Fast Talk, Fist/Punch, Grapple, Handgun, Head Butt, Kick, Other Language, Persuade, Psychology.

Scholarly Pursuits

THIS HEADING COVERS a range of pursuits all having in common higher, technical education or the equivalent in real experience. Opportunities for involvement in arcane mysteries are abundant. Scholars peruse old tomes, explore forgotten lands, and maintain correspondences with a wide variety of people.

For purposes of definition, scholarly pursuits are divided into three broad categories: Humanities, Sciences, and Engineering. Pursuits in Humanities include anthropology, archaeology, history and languages, as well as art, literature, drama, and others. Sciences include astronomy, biology, chemistry, geology, pharmacy, physics, psychology, as well as their various offshoots, sub-sciences, and combinations. Engineering includes both mechanical and electrical engineering plus architectural engineering and mathematics. The relatively new field of radio engineering is also included in this group.

Professor

Many scholars find occupations within the education industry. Others prefer to work in the private sector, employed by large corporations. A few are independent

Anthropologist Margaret Murray (1863-1963)

Margaret Murray was a British anthropologist whose primary fields of study were Egyptology and the history of witchcraft. Her best-known book, *The Witch-Cult in Western Europe* (1921), relates her findings and theories on the latter subject. In it Dr. Murray claims that witchcraft is actually an ancient fertility cult that worships a god possessed of two forms: one a horned male figure, the other a female huntress a la the Greek Artemis and the Roman Diana. According to Murray, this cult originated in western Europe thousands of years before Christ with a race of dwarves who were driven underground with the coming of Man. These creatures survived as the faeries and elves of European folklore. The surviving witch-cults are not evil, spell casting hags but followers of their spiritual leader, the earth goddess/huntress Diana/Artemis. When first published, Murray's findings gained little acceptance in academic circles, but the book spurred a pagan revival in England and Europe. She later published two other books of a similar nature.

scholars, able to support themselves through publications, speaking engagements, grants, private funding, sales of patents, or occasional free lance commissions from private companies.

Student/Intern

This character may be a student enrolled at a college or university, or the employee of a company receiving minimal compensation but valuable on-the-job training.

EARNINGS: Pauper to Upper Lower class.

CONTACTS AND CONNECTIONS: Access to professors, laboratories, libraries, and other facilities.

SKILLS: English, Library Use, and up to three fields of study.

SPECIAL: +1 to EDU.

Professor/Teacher

Professors are employed by colleges and universities; teachers work in public and private schools with the lower grades. Occasionally larger corporations employ a teacher to train employees, give seminars, or write technical publications. Independent scholars sometimes support themselves by teaching part-time courses at colleges.

EARNINGS: Lower Middle to Upper Middle class.

CONTACTS AND CONNECTIONS: Scholars within your specialty, universities and libraries. Near unrestricted use of libraries, laboratories, and other university facilities.

SKILLS: Credit Rating, English, Library Use, Persuade, and up to three fields of study.

SPECIAL: +2 to EDU. Add 10 points to Credit Rating.

Researcher

The academic world sponsors a good deal of research, particularly in the fields of astronomy, physics, and other theoretical sciences. The private sector employs thousands of researchers, especially chemists, pharmacists, and engineers. The big oil companies hire many geologists. Researchers spend their time indoors, working and writing.

EARNINGS: Lower Middle to Upper Middle class.

CONTACTS AND CONNECTIONS: Other scholars in your field; access to corporation libraries and laboratories; possible funding for pet projects.

SKILLS: Credit Rating, English, Library Use, and up to three fields of study.

SPECIAL: +3 to EDU.

Archaeologist Howard Carter (1873-1939)

Carter was a British archaeologist whose fame was made certain by his discovery of the tomb of the Pharaoh Tutankhamen in 1922. Carter led many expeditions to Egypt's Valley of the Kings, and for a time directed Egypt's program to preserve its ancient artifacts. His father, an artist, taught him draftsmanship, and in 1891 he went to Egypt as a draftsman on an archaeological survey. A year later he received his first formal training in archaeology at Tell el Amarna, under the tutelage of the prominent British archaeologist Sir Flinders Petrie. Carter's discoveries over the next thirty years included the tombs of Thutmose IV, Queen Hashepsut, and Amenhotep I. Among Carter's many books on his discoveries is the three-volume *The Tomb of Tut-ankh-amen*. Proponents of the "curse of King Tut's tomb" neglect to note that Carter, the man truly responsible for the tomb's "looting," lives for seventeen years after the invoking of the "curse."

Researcher George Washington Carver (1859?-1943)

Carver was born to slave parents in Missouri, going on to become an internationally famous agricultural researcher. He attended Simpson College in Indianola, Iowa, earning his way by working various menial jobs. Carver later graduated from Iowa State College in 1894, where he took a post as assistant botanist. He started a fungus collection that eventually boasted 20,000 separate species. Carver transferred to Alabama's Tuskegee Institute in 1896 at the invitation of Booker T. Washington. Here he revolutionized Southern agriculture, urging farmers to grow peanuts, sweet potatoes, and other crops, in place of cotton. Carver derived over three hundred products from the peanut, including peanut butter, ink, and instant "coffee." Sweet potatoes yielded another hundred-plus products, and pecans over seventy more. He invented a number of other ingenious products from unlikely sources. In 1916 Carver was made a Fellow in the Royal Society of Arts in London, an accomplishment few Americans could boast of. By the time of his death, eighteen schools had been named in his honor.

Field Researcher

Field researchers are usually highly experienced, independent and resourceful, and most often robust and healthy. Oil companies send geologists into the field to explore potential petroleum fields, anthropologists study primitive tribes in forgotten corners of the globe, and archaeologists spend years of their lives unearthing treasures in deserts and jungles, bargaining with native diggers and governments.

EARNINGS: Middle to Upper Middle class.

CONTACTS AND CONNECTIONS: Other scholars in your field, grant foundations, news media, foreign government officials, corporate sponsors, patrons.

SKILLS: Accounting, Bargain, Climb, Credit Rating, First Aid, Jump, Library Use, Other Language, Persuade, and up three fields of study.

SPECIAL: +2 to EDU and +1 to CON. Add 20 bonus points to Credit Rating.

Miscellaneous Occupations

THE FOLLOWING OCCUPATIONS include those that do not seem to smoothly fit under other headings. Nonetheless, they offer some of the more interesting possibilities for character development. Most suggest obvious opportunities for the character to get involved in dark secrets.

Antique Dealer

Antique dealers may own their own shop, retail items out of their homes, or go on extended buying trips and making profit on resales to urban stores.

EARNINGS: Lower Middle to Upper Middle class.

CONTACTS AND CONNECTIONS: Local historians, antique dealers.

SKILLS: Accounting, Bargain, Credit Rating, Drive Auto, Fast Talk, History, Library Use, Navigate, Persuade.

SPECIAL: +1 to EDU. 1D20+40 points in Antiques skill.

Book Dealer

A book dealer may be the owner of a retail outlet or specialize in buying trips across the country and even overseas. Some represent wealthy clients at book auctions held in England and other places.

EARNINGS: Upper Lower to Middle class.

CONTACTS AND CONNECTIONS: Bibliographers, book dealers, libraries and universities, possibly major clients.

SKILLS: Accounting, Bargain, Credit Rating, Drive Auto, English, History, Library Use, Navigate, Other Language, Persuade.

SPECIAL: +1 to EDU. 1D20+40 points in Bookbinding/Printing History skill.

Dilettante

Dilettantes are self-supporting, living off an inheritance, trust fund, or other. The amount of money at your disposal may be great or meager but is enough to keep you from being forced to seek employment.

EARNINGS: Upper Lower to Wealthy.

CONTACTS AND CONNECTIONS: Variable, but usually people of your own background and tastes. You may be a member of the local Masonic lodge or other fraternal organization. Or your tastes may be more bohemian, calling for an assortment of artists and poets among your acquaintances.

SKILLS: Credit Rating, plus up to four areas of interest.

Fireman

Firemen are civil servants, employed by the communities they serve. They work around the clock, on shifts lasting several days: eating, sleeping, and entertaining themselves within the confines of the station.

Hobo

Organized along military lines, promotion through lieutenant, captain, and chief is possible.

EARNINGS: Lower Middle to Upper Middle class.

CONTACTS AND CONNECTIONS: A few civic amenities.

SKILLS: Axe, Climb, Dodge, First Aid, Jump, Roping.

SPECIAL: +1 to STR and +1 to CON. Special skill, Fire Fighting, of 1D20+40 points.

Flapper

Being a flapper is a state of mind rather than an occupation, although some dilettantes have raised it to a fine art. Pixie haircuts, cloche hats, long strings of beads, and gowns slit high up the side are *de rigueur*. Above all is required a distinct lack of restraint. Flappers are most often employed as secretaries, sales help, or other, similar work.

Many origins are given for the name flapper, but it most likely dates back to the early years of the decade when it became fashionable to wear rubber galoshes left unbuckled to 'flap' while walking.

EARNINGS: Upper Lower to Lower Middle class.

CONTACTS AND CONNECTIONS: Variable.

SKILLS: Bargain, Fast Talk, Persuade, Psychology, plus possible employment skills.

SPECIAL: +2 APP.

Gardener/Grave Digger

These characters are strong, healthy types--most often loners. They occasionally surprise people with an unexpected knowledge of literature, philosophy, poetry, or other self-taught specialty.

EARNINGS: Upper Lower to Lower class.

CONTACTS AND CONNECTIONS: None.

SKILLS: Bargain, plus up to three areas of interest.

SPECIAL: +1 to STR and +1 to CON. Immune to sanity losses from visiting graveyards at night, unearthing graves, etc.

Hobo

Although there are people out of work and, as always, alcoholics lying in the gutters, the true hobo forms a separate breed. Riding the rails continually, on the move from one town to another and working only when necessary, they are poets and vagabonds--adventurers, criminals, and thieves.

EARNINGS: Pauper.

CONTACTS AND CONNECTIONS: Other hobos, a few friendly railroad guards, soft touches in numerous towns.

SKILLS: Bargain, Climb, Fast Talk, Hide, Jump, Listen, Natural History, Sneak, Spot Hidden, Persuade.

Hobo Woodie Guthrie (1912-1967)

Woodrow Wilson Guthrie's fame does not come until the 1940s and afterward, but his experiences during the late 1920s and throughout the Depression era fueled the songs that made him famous. Woodie Guthrie was born in Oklahoma; his father was a sometime musician and professional boxer. Woodie left home at the age of sixteen and, in 1929, while visiting an uncle in Texas, learned to play the guitar. When the depression hit, he rode the rails, living as a hobo and eking out a little money playing his songs. Guthrie's songs were part folk song, part social commentary. In 1937 he took a job at a radio station in Los Angeles. His music had been recorded only casually in the 1940s, but his songs grew in popularity; Guthrie even recorded with legendary bluesmen such as Leadbelly. He moved to New York just before the Second World War, where he met up with other folk musicians, and where he became a communist for a short time. During the war Guthrie served in the merchant marine. After the war, Guthrie was mistakenly diagnosed as an alcoholic; his true malady was a nervous disorder which kept him institutionalized for much of the last fifteen years of his life. Guthrie's autobiography, *Bound for Glory*, is published in 1943.

SPECIAL: Hobos have a special written language of signs and symbols. These unobtrusive messages, scratched on walls and rocks, warn of vicious dogs and sadistic railroad guards, or inform as to where to get a good meal or find a place to sleep.

Librarian

Librarians are most often employed by public institutions or universities. Occasionally opportunities appear to take over custodial care of a private library, but these are increasingly infrequent.

EARNINGS: Lower Middle to Middle class.

CONTACTS AND CONNECTIONS: Few.

SKILLS: Accounting, English, Library Use, Other Language, and up to three favorite reading topics.

SPECIAL: +2 to EDU. Bonus 20 points added to Library Use.

Merchant Marine

These are the sailors who work the cargo ships of America and the rest of the world. They are protected by a seaman's union but once away from port are truly at the mercy of the ship's captain. Although many of the gross abuses of the past have ceased, it is still a coarse and demanding life.

Sailors work aboard ships usually one voyage at a time. A small advance is paid upon sailing, the rest due when the ship lands in port. After parting with a ship, sailors typically spend the next few days, weeks, or months ashore, spending all their money. When finally broke they seek out the next ship leaving port and sign on.

EARNINGS: Upper Lower class.

CONTACTS AND CONNECTIONS: Seaman's union, smugglers.

SKILLS: Anthropology, Climb, Electrical Repair, Jump, Mechanical Repair, Operate Heavy Machinery, Other Language.

SPECIAL: +1 to STR and CON. -2 to EDU.

Museum Curator

A museum curator can be responsible for a large facility like a university or other publicly funded institution, or any sort of smaller museum, often specializing in local geology or other such topic.

EARNINGS: Upper Lower to Upper Middle class.

CONTACTS AND CONNECTIONS: Local universities and scholars, publishers, museum patrons.

SKILLS: Accounting, Bargain, Credit Rating, English, Library Use, Persuade.

Occultist

Occultists are students of magic and other powers. They fully believe in extra normal abilities and actively attempt to discover these powers within themselves. Most are familiar with a broad range of different philosophies and magical theories.

EARNINGS: Pauper to Lower class.

CONTACTS AND CONNECTIONS: Libraries, occult societies. other occultists.

SKILLS: Anthropology, English, History, Library Use, Occult, Other Language.

Parapsychologist

Parapsychologists do not pretend to enjoy extraordinary powers, but instead spend their efforts attempting to observe, record, and study such instances. Making use of a few simple devices and a good dose of common sense, they spend a major portion of their time debunking fake mediums and mistaken phenomena than recording actual evidence. Some make intensive studies of ESP, telekinesis, and other paranormal powers.

EARNINGS: Upper Lower to Lower Middle class.

CONTACTS AND CONNECTIONS: Universities, parapsychological publications.

SKILLS: Anthropology, Electrical Repair, Hypnotism, Library Use, Mechanical Repair, Occult, Photography.

Surveyor

Unless one is lucky enough to land a steady job with a large city or building contractor, a surveyor has to stay on the move, traveling from town to town, state to state, in search of work.

EARNINGS: Upper Lower to Middle class.

CONTACTS AND CONNECTIONS: State and local records offices.

SKILLS: Accounting, Bargain, Library Use, Natural History, Navigate, Photography, Spot Hidden.

Parapsychologist Harry Price (1881-1948)

Price was a tireless British parapsychologist. A member of the British Society for Psychical Research (founded in 1882), Price formed his own similar organization, the National Laboratory of Psychical Research, in 1926. Price's interest in the occult started early--he is said to have investigated his first paranormal case (a poltergeist) at the age of fifteen. He had no scientific background or academic credentials to speak of, but he was a skilled magician, and used this talent to spot would-be frauds. He was adept at generating publicity for his experiments and findings, and his outspokenness make him many enemies among psychics, mediums, and academics. Whatever his faults, Price was a meticulous researcher, always making careful preparations to spot frauds at seances and at sites of alleged paranormal activity. He uses cameras with infrared film, motion-detecting devices, and a well-stocked "ghost-hunter's kit" in his investigations. Price conducted many seances in the 1920s, and investigated instances of poltergeist activity, ghostly hauntings, and psychokinesis. In 1929 he became engaged in his most famous case: the haunting of Borley Rectory, northeast of London. Price devoted more than seventeen years to his study of this apparently genuine haunting, and wrote two books about it. All told, he wrote seventeen books throughout his career.

Occultist A.E. Waite (1857-1942)

Arthur Edward Waite is one of the most famous and studious turn-of-the-century occultists. Waite was born in Brooklyn, the son of a ship's captain. His father died when he was two years old and the family moved to England to be with his mother's family. Brought up Catholic, Waite turned to spiritualism in 1874, when his sister died. When he found the spiritualists wanting, he joined H.P. Blavatsky's Theosophical Society, and studied alchemy and the mysticism of the French occultist Eliphas Levi. His first book, *The Mysteries of Magic* (1886), dealt with Levi's writings. A year later, while researching in the British Museum, Waite met fellow author and mystic Arthur Machen, who would be his friend and occasional co-author until Waite's death. In 1891 Waite joined a new society of occultists, the Hermetic Order of the Golden Dawn. He would be involved in the Dawn's various incarnations off and on until 1914; Waite would in fact lead one faction of the Golden Dawn from 1903-1914, reorganizing its magical curriculum along more Christian lines. Though he himself claimed to be skeptical of its usefulness, Waite designed what is still the most widely used Tarot deck--the Rider-Waite or Rider Tarot deck; he wrote *The Pictorial Key to the Tarot* as a companion to this deck.

Undertaker

Undertakers are licensed by the state. They either own their own funeral parlors or work for someone who does.

EARNINGS: Lower Middle to Upper Middle class.

CONTACTS AND CONNECTIONS: Few.

SKILLS: Accounting, Bargain, Biology, Credit Rating, Persuade, Psychology.

SPECIAL: Considering the nature of the undertaker's work, certain sanity losses regarding corpses, blood, or accident victims might be safely reduced or ignored.

Zookeeper

Zoos are a fixture in all large U.S. cities and many medium-sized ones. Zookeepers are responsible for the feeding and care of the animals; grounds keepers and attendants take care of other chores.

EARNINGS: Lower Middle to Middle class.

CONTACTS AND CONNECTIONS: Local university zoology department.

SKILLS: Accounting, Biology, First Aid, Natural History, Medicine (veterinary), Pharmacy.

■

Skills for the 1920s

THE FOLLOWING SKILL descriptions are reprinted from *Call of Cthulhu* Fifth Edition for the convenience of players. Boxed material contains extra information pertinent to the era.

Skill Levels

Though not an official part of the rules it is sometimes handy to judge a character's ability according to the level of their skill rather than resorting to dice rolling. The following 'levels' are offered as suggestions only and should not be taken literally in all instances.

20-25%: A novice or beginner--the basic starting percentage for most learned skills. A basic level allows a character to operate machinery or equipment in a safe manner under normal circumstances; speak a language well enough to find their way around a foreign country, order dinner, etc.; make routine repairs; or function as an assistant or apprentice in a job position.

50%: The usual minimum required for a professional to gain and keep employment, be it as a lawyer, doctor, archaeologist, car mechanic, taxi driver, or mail pilot. This level of skill in a foreign language allows one to carry on normal conversation, read books, etc.

75%: This level indicates notable ability. In a professional skill this person would qualify as a director or other type of supervisor. A 75% or higher skill allows a character to read even the most difficult books, and effect reliable, accurate translations. Professional race drivers, stunt pilots, or athletes will all demonstrate pertinent skill of 75% or more.

90%: Skills at this level or above indicate world-class abilities. A character with such a skill level might discover a cure for a known disease, become a world-renowned flying ace or race driver, or write a significant piece of literature in a foreign language. However, this is only a measure of potential, not actuality. A character must still do something to earn such recognition.

■ ACCOUNTING (10%)

Grants understanding of accountancy procedures, and reveals the financial functioning of a business or person. Inspecting the books, one might detect cheated employees, siphoned-off funds, payment of bribes or blackmail, and whether or not the financial condition is better or worse than claimed. Looking through old accounts, one could see how money was gained or lost in the past (grain, slave-trading, whiskey-running, etc.) and to whom and for what payment was made.

1920S Accounting

1929 saw the publication of *The Economics of Accountancy* by J.B. Canning. It marks one of the first attempts to build a structure of accounting on the basis of modern economic theory.

As with most professions, a skill of 50% or more is usually the minimum required to qualify an individual as a professional. An investigator with a skill of 75 or more could be a CPA (a Certified Public Accountant), and a skill of 90 or more might allow him to function as an actuary.

■ ANTHROPOLOGY (00%)

Enables the user to identify an individual's way of life from his behavior. If the skill-user observes another culture from within for a time, or works from accurate records concerning an extinct culture, he or she may make simple predictions about that culture's mores and morals, even though the evidence may be incomplete. Studying the culture for a month or more, the anthropologist understands how the culture functions and in combination with Psychology, may predict the actions and beliefs of a representative from it. Essentially useful only with existing cultures.

1920s Anthropology

By the 1920s anthropology has clearly divided itself into two disciplines: cultural anthropology and physical anthropology, each subdivided differently in the U.S and in Europe.

Numerous books of interest have been lately published, including: Franz Boas' *The Mind of Primitive Man* (1911); Bronislaw Malinowski's *The Argonauts of the Western Pacific* (1922) and *Customs and Crimes in Savage Society* (1926); J.G. Frazer's *Totemism and Exogamy* (1910) and *Folklore in the Old Testament* (1918); Max Schmidt's *The Primitive Races of Mankind* (1926); and Margaret Mead's *The Coming of Age in Samoa* (1928).

In 1927, remains of Peking Man are unearthed in China.

■ ARCHAEOLOGY (00%)

Allows dating and identification of artifacts from past cultures and the detecting of fakes. Having thoroughly inspected a site, the user might deduce the purposes and way of life of those who left the remains. Anthropology might aid in this. Archaeologists specialize in particular cultures and periods.

Although a long-standing archaeological interest in Egypt has been further spurred by the discovery of Tutankhamen's tomb in 1922, other parts of the world are now seeing scrutiny. Hiram Bingham discovers the Incan city of Machu Picchu in 1911, while in the early 1920s excavations at Mohenjo-Daro and Harappa lead to the discovery of the ancient Indus civilization. Stonhenge is dated for the first time, to 4000 years ago, and by the end of the decade the remains of the prehistoric Shang civilization are discovered at An-Yang in eastern China.

1920s Archaeology

Numerous archaeological societies exist, most publishing their own journals. Some of the oldest and best know are: The Hellenic Society, the Egypt Exploration Society, and the Palestine Exploration Fund.

■ ART (05%)

Specify song, some musical instrument, painting, cooking, etc.--any non-literary art which a creative person might seriously pursue through life. With a success, the performance or creation is pleasing and the audience is satisfied. Failure indicates that the artist was off-key or inexpressive. Lovecraft's artists invoke the traditional muses, but the keeper might allow much wider definitions of 'art,' from baseball to juggling. The player should note the style or medium: opera singer, *oil* painter, etc. The investigator sheet contains blank spaces for different versions of this skill.

1920s Art

Max Ernst is a leading dadaist painter and sculptor. Politically outspoken Mexican painter Diego Rivera has a showing in New York. Picasso explores cubism. Bela Bartok visits U.S. in 1927. Classical guitarist André Segovia debuts in Paris. Arturo Toscanini picks up the conductor's baton at the New York Philharmonic in 1928. Pablo Casals is the world's leading cellist.

■ ASTRONOMY (00%)

The user knows or knows how to find out which stars and planets are overhead at a particular day or hour of day or night, when eclipses and meteor showers occur, and the names of important stars. An academic might be able to calculate orbits or discuss stellar life cycles.

1920s Astronomy

America's leading astronomer is Edwin Hubble who, in 1922-24, discovered that nebulae are actually separate galaxies lying far beyond the Milky Way. His discovery in 1929 of 'red shifts' leads to theories about an expanding, and ever-dynamic universe. Astronomer Clyde Tombaugh discovers the ninth planet of our solar system in 1931, naming it Pluto.

The largest telescopes in the world are the 100-inch reflector on Mt. Wilson near Pasadena, California, and a 72-inch reflector in Vancouver, British Columbia. Plans for larger instruments are currently being laid, including the 200-inch reflector to be installed atop Mt. Palomar.

A number of Astronomical societies exist, publishing journals and newsletters. These include: The Royal Astronomical Society (1820); The British Astronomical Society (1869); The American Astronomical Society (1899); The Astronomical Society of the Pacific (1880); and The American Association of Variable Star Observers (1911). All welcome the amateur astronomer.

■ BARGAIN (05%)

The skill of obtaining something for an agreeable price. The bargainer must state the price at which he wishes to purchase the item and, for each 2% difference between that price and the asking price, he must subtract 1 percentile from his Bargain skill. The seller will not take a loss, no matter how well he or she Bargains, but the keeper usually determines the bottom-line amount secretly.

By implication, use this skill in any negotiation which features an exchange of value. Combination rolls with Credit Rating, Fast Talk, or Persuade might help in bargaining.

A simple Bargain may be struck in a few minutes. A complex contract might take weeks, and Bargain might them work in combination with Law.

1920s Bargain

Current well-known American philanthropists--most with established grant foundations--include: Andrew Carnegie, George Eastman, Henry Ford, Daniel Guggenheim, Andrew Mellon, Julius Rosenwald, and J.P. Morgan (the younger).

■ BIOLOGY (00%)

The science of life, including botany, cytology, ecology, genetics, histology, microbiology, physiology, zoology, and so on. the investigator's understanding reflects the era of play. With this skill one might for instance develop a vaccine against some hideous Mythos bacterium, or isolate the hallucinogenic properties of a rare plant.

1920s Biology

By the 1920s, a division of roles has occurred: molecular biology, microbiology, biochemistry, and biophysics, being only a few among the many. *The Science and Philosophy of the Organism* (1929) by Hans Driesch is an up-to-date reference. The Lister Institute, funded by Irish beer baron Edward Guiness, is currently establishing a 'library' of over 2000 living cultures including bacteria, protozoa, and fungi.

■ CHEMISTRY (00%)

A study of the composition of substances, the effects of temperature, energy, and pressure upon them, and how they affect one another. With Chemistry, one might create or extract complex chemical compounds, including simple explosives, poisons, gases, and acids, requiring at least a day or so with the proper equipment and chemicals. The user could also analyze an unknown substance, given proper equipment and reagents.

1920s Chemistry

By the 1920s Chemistry has become an essential part of most sciences from medicine and pharmacy, to physics and biology. Synthetic substances like Bakelite--the first plastic--are being developed, while chemistry also helps to explain the role of vitamins and hormones. Synthetic replacement medicines, such as Novocaine for cocaine, are being developed, as well as faster film emulsions and stronger alloys.

Currently, there are 92 elements listed on the Periodic Table.

■ CLIMB (40%)

Climb is self-explanatory. A successful Climb roll must be made every 10 to 30 feet, depending on the difficulty of the climb that the keeper perceives. Various conditions--surface, wind, day or night, rain, etc.--may be factors.

If an investigator needs to climb quietly, match the player's D100 roll against both Climb and Sneak. If succeeding in Climb but failing in Sneak, he or she climbed successfully, but made noise. If the Climb failed but the Sneak succeeded, he or she fell without important noise.

■ CONCEAL (15%)

Allows the visual covering up, secreting, or masking of an object or objects, perhaps with debris, cloth, or other intervening or illusion-promoting materials, perhaps by making a secret panel or false compartment, or perhaps by repainting or otherwise changing an item's characteristics to escape detection.

With it, a person might be secreted from sight, but could not be disguised to evade even a cursory inspection. Larger objects of any sort should be increasingly hard to conceal. Things larger than elephants should not be concealable by a person, though they might be by a group.

■ CREDIT RATING (15%)

Narrowly, how prosperous and confident the investigator seems to be. This is the investigator's chance to panhandle or get a loan from a bank or business, and it is also the chance for the investigator to pass a bad check or to bluff past a demand for credentials.

In small towns everyone knows everyone, and Credit Rating amounts to an index of personal reputation as well as monetary worth. Thus Credit Rating might ebb and flow because of scandal or personal behavior, while the loss or accumulation of money effects minor change or no change. As appropriate, the keeper may cause a character to make clear such distinctions.

■ CTHULHU MYTHOS (00%)

Secrets man was not meant to know.

■ DODGE (DEX x2%)

Allows an investigator to instinctively evade seen blows, thrown missiles, ambushes, and so forth. A character attempting Dodge may perform no attacks in that combat round, but may parry.

An investigator can try to dodge something if it can be seen coming from a distance--a rolling rock or swerving automobile, for instance--and can try to get out of the way.

Dodge can increase through experience, like other skills.

■ DRIVE AUTOMOBILE (20%)

Anyone with this skill can drive a car or light truck, and make ordinary maneuvers and cope with ordinary vehicle problems. If the investigator wants to lose a pursuer or trail someone, both participants might attempt Driving rolls until one fails and the other succeeds. Dangerous maneuvers always call for Drive rolls.

Drive Carriage is a similar skill starting at 00%.

1920s Drive Automobile

Drivers are licensed by individual states. Most require a minimum age of 16, although there are exceptions, especially regarding the use of farm vehicles by underage persons in conjunction with the work of the farm. To obtain a license a short, simple written test must first be passed, followed by a brief road test in the presence of a police officer. Passing both tests, and the payment of a fee, results in a license usually good for one to two years before needing renewal. Driver's licenses are valid in other states, but can be revoked by a judge if the driver is repeatedly ticketed for unsafe practices.

■ ELECTRICAL REPAIR (10%)

Enables the investigator to repair or alter electrical equipment such as auto ignitions, electric motors, and burglar alarms. To fix an electrical device may require special parts or tools.

1920s Electrical Repair

Most repair jobs in the early 1920s require only a knowledge of motors and generators, lighting and heating systems, and the comparatively simple circuitry of automobiles and burglar alarms. These sorts of tasks could logically be handled by Mechanical Repair and it is suggested that the one skill be used for both mechanical and simple electrical repairs. By the end of the decade, however, the radio business is booming and television already in its infancy. Repairing these devices calls for an Electronics skill.

Numerous schools and correspondence courses currently abound, offering to teach these 'vital new skills'; even courses on television are available. *Popular Science* and *Modern Electronics* (the latter founded in 1908 by Hugo Gernsback) are both monthly periodicals devoted to new developments in technology.

■ FAST TALK (05%)

Causes the target to agree as the user wishes. Without reflecting, the target signs the paper, allows the trespass, loans the automobile, or whatever else within reason is asked. But given a short time to think and a successful Idea roll, the target comes to his or her senses: the Fast Talk loses effect.

In a game minute or so, Fast Talk may pass off suspect goods and facts as reliable or as not worth bothering about. In contrast, Persuade and Bargain may take hours or days to conclude. Fast Talk is quick to take effect, but it can be used at most on a handful of people. Fast Talk will not work on targets whose minds are made up; use Persuade instead.

1920s Fast Talk

The 1920s are the heyday of the scam artist, the con-game, and the flim-flam man. In 1921 Oscar Hartzell begins expanding his 'Drake Fortune' scam, which eventually reaches international proportions. Pinkerton warns of a nationwide ring passing bad checks at banks. In 1922 Joseph "Yellow Kid" Weil and a partner pull of a $300,000 bank scam. The Yellow Kid surfaces later that year, running a fake medium hustle. 1922 also finds Victor "The Count" Lustig (who has already sold the Eiffel Tower--twice) swindling a bank out of $10,000. Insurance and real estate scams proliferate. In 1923 Frederick A. Cooke, a claimant to the discovery of the North Pole, is convicted in a Texas oil-lease fraud. In 1924 worthless stocks flood the Midwest and the Yellow Kid bilks twenty suckers in Chicago out of $500,000. Victor Lustig shows up in Chicago in 1925 and before leaving, nips gangster Al Capone for 5 G's. In 1927 Walter Hohenau stings investors with the latest in 'water-to-gas' schemes.

■ FIRST AID (30%)

The percentage chance of awakening an unconscious or stunned comrade, setting a broken limb, treating burn damage, resuscitating a drowning victim, etc. First Aid has no effect on diseases or subtle physical ailments, nor on poisoning unless the keeper admits the roll. Treated with First Aid, an investigator's healing rate stays a 1D3 points per week. Moved to a hospital and successfully treated with Medicine, that rate rises to 2D3 per week.

Failure in applying first Aid requires the user wait some reasonable amount of time to try again, but another practitioner could make his or her attempt in the next round.

A success with this skill allows the user to immediately heal 1D3 hit points of a single attack or injury. Thus an investigator suffering multiple gunshot wounds might receive First Aid for each, as long as they were not incurred in the same attack. One could get more detailed in listing wounds and injuries, of course, but the bookkeeping might be tedious.

In the same or the succeeding combat round, an investigator who has just died may be returned to life if the emergency 1D3 hit points raises his or her hit point total to at least +1.

A success with First Aid immediately awakens any victim of a knock-out attack and, if the keeper wishes anyone unconscious.

Once an investigator has had First Aid successfully applied to an injury, further applications either of First Aid or of Medicine have no effect. A new injury could be treated independently, however. An application of the skill takes a combat round, or as the keeper determines. See also Medicine.

1920s First Aid

First Aid kits of the time typically include: bandages, gauze, scissors, needle and thread, olive oil, Epsom salts, powdered mustard, Witch Hazel, oil of cloves, syrup of ipecac, collodion, and lime-water. Iodine is the best topical antiseptic. Note that snake bite antivenins are not yet available.

■ FIST/PUNCH (50%)

A self-explanatory skill, which might be depicted as a closed fist, a karate chop, a roundhouse punch, a violent slap, etc. One can use Fist/Punch to parry Kick and Head Butt. Martial Arts can add to its impact, and the knock-out rule can be applied to it.

1920s Fist/Punch

Brass knuckles add 2 points of damage to every hit (3 if spiked), but are illegal in most states either specifically, or as concealed weapons.

■ GEOLOGY (00%)

Enables an investigator to tell the approximate age of a rock stratum, recognize fossil types, distinguish many minerals and crystals, locate promising sites for drilling, evaluate soils, and anticipate volcanism, seismic, events, avalanches, and other such phenomena. Sherlock Holmes was expert in London-are soils, and could trace a man's movements by studying the dirt on his boots.

1920s Geology

The theory of floating continents (tectonics) gains credence in this decade as favorable evidence continues to accumulate. A group of American geologists put forth the theory that periodic flooding in parts of the world may have been the result of ocean levels rising and falling due to periodic ice ages, rather than a lifting and settling of the continents as previously believed.

The world's two best-known societies are: The Geological Society of London (1807); and The Geology Society of America (1888) in New York.

■ GRAPPLE (25%)

A Grapple is a special personal attack, frequently chosen to harmlessly subdue an opponent. This attack may be parried by a countering successful Grapple or other attack by the target, but only in the first round of attack.

If a Grapple attack succeeds in the first round and is not neutralized, then the attacker holds the target and may thereafter exercise one of several options.

Immobilize the target by overcoming the target's STR with his or her own STR, using the Resistance Table. With a success, the target is held fast indefinitely, until the grappler attempts another action.

Knock down the target. If used, this option automatically succeeds.

Knock out the target in the first or a later round: see the knock-out rule.

Disarm the target. With successful Grapples in consecutive rounds, an investigator could Grapple to prevent a hand-to-hand attack in the first round and then seize the weapon or weapon hand in the second round.

Physically injure the target. The opponent already must be successfully grappled. The grappler must receive a second successful Grapple roll in the first round, or a successful Grapple in some later round. Success costs the target 1D6 hit points plus the attacker's damage bonus. Harm in subsequent rounds requires a new Grapple success in those rounds, and the injury done remains the same.

Strangle the target. Beginning in the round stated, the target begins to asphyxiate, as per the Drowning rules, and continues in subsequent rounds. the attacker needs no further Grapple rolls.

In either type of injury-making Grapple, the victim is caught and can escape only by successfully matching STR against STR on the Resistance Table on his DEX rank.

1920s Grapple

World heavyweight wrestling champions of the decade include: Gus Sonneberg, Joe Stecher, Stanislaus Zbyszko, and Ed "Strangler" Lewis.

■ HANDGUN (20%)

Use for all pistol-like firearms when firing discrete shots.

■ HEAD BUTT (10%)

The essential barroom brawl skill, Head Butt is applied to the belly of an opponent or else to his temple, crown, nose, chin, or back of the head. This personal attack can be made in cramped surroundings, and part of its effect comes from its surprising quickness. One cannot parry with Head Butt, but Martial Arts can add to its effect, and the knock-out rule can be applied to it.

■ HIDE (10%)

As opposed to Conceal, Hide concerns the individual user's ability to escape detection in an unprepared position. Use this skill only in a pursuit situation, or when under surveillance or patrol. It lets the user choose objects, bushes, deep shadows, etc., in which to lurk for a while. Cover must be present. In an area being watched, the user can move while hiding. Figure the chance for successful movement by halving the Hide skill amount.

■ HISTORY (20%)

Enables an investigator to remember the history of a country, city, or region, with particular reference to pertinent events. Lessen the chance if the investigator needs to remember a particularly obscure fact. A successful History roll might be used to help identify written forms of extinct human languages or to know some ancient technique.

1920s History

H.G Wells' Outline of History (1920, revised 1931) is the popular favorite. Academics and others are attracted to Oswald Spengler's Decline of the West (translated 1926-28).

■ JUMP (25%)

With a success, the investigator can leap up vertically and grab to his or her own height, safely leap down vertically to own height, jump horizontally from a standing start to own height across a gap, or run and jump horizontally to twice own height. If falling from a height, a successful Jump subtracts 1D6 hit points from those lost to the injury.

1920s Jump

World record jumps in the latter part of the 1920s are as follows: Running High Jump, 6 feet, 8 1/4 inches; Running Long Jump, 25 feet, 10 7/8 inches; Standing Long Jump 8 feet, 5 1/2 inches; Pole Vault, 14 feet.

■ KICK (25%)

Whether a straight-forward kick to the groin or the jaw, or an elegant flying kick, or a kick with both legs while lying on a floor, a Kick is powerful enough to do damage wherever it lands. A Kick may parry and Martial Arts may add to its effectiveness, but do not apply the knock-out rule to Kick except in special circumstances.

1920s Kick

The damage figure of 1D6 assumes hard-soled, leather shoes; add 1 point if boots are steel-toed, or particularly pointed such as cowboy boots. Reduce damage if softer shoes are worn: slippers, pumps, etc.

■ LAW (05%)

Represents an investigator's chance of knowing a pertinent law, precedent, legal maneuver, or court procedure. In another country, halve the chance for success with this skill, unless he or she has spent 30-INT studying that nation's law.

1920s Law

In a landmark case, Clarence Darrow loses the Scopes Monkey Trial in Tennessee to William Jennings Bryan in 1925.

■ LIBRARY USE (25%)

In many ways it is the most important skill in the game. Library Use enables an investigator to find a given book, newspaper, or reference in a library or collection of documents, assuming that the item is there. Each use of this skill marks four hours of continuous search. An investigator rarely gets more than two tries per day.

This skill can locate a locked-case or rare-book special collection, but Fast Talk, Persuade, Bargain, Credit Rating, a bribe, or special credentials might be needed to get at the books.

1920s Library Use

Public libraries abound in the 1920s, even in small towns where many of them were funded by the Carnegie Institute and other organizations. Although readily available, their resources are limited. Most large American cities have creditable public collections, particularly New York and Boston. Universities maintain large libraries, some of them with renowned collections. Although borrowing is limited, most offer access to the public, whether enrolled in the school or not.

■ LISTEN (25%)

Measures the ability of an investigator to interpret and understand sound, including overheard conversations, mutters behind a closed door, and whispered words in a cafe. The keeper may use it to determine the course of an impending encounter: was your investigator awakened by that crackling twig?

1920s Listen

A good quality stethoscope can be of use when listening through walls, etc. Microphones of day are large and difficult to conceal. Phone taps are easily made, most often at the line's connection to the outdoor pole.

■ LOCKSMITH (00%)

The user may repair locks, make keys, or open locks with the aid of skeleton keys, picks, and other tools. Especially difficult locks may lower the chance for success. A locksmith can open car doors, library windows, Chinese puzzle boxes, etc., and penetrate simple alarm systems. Sophisticated safes, vaults, and other serious defensive systems are beyond this skill. Keepers might combine Locksmith with DEX or POW rolls to cover a variety of surreptitious situations.

1920s Locksmith

Although cheaper combination locks can sometimes be 'felt' and opened successfully, higher quality combinations found on safes and vaults are impervious to this method. The usual method is to steal the entire safe, taking it to a safe location where time can be spent 'peeling' it with torches, crowbars, and hammers. Large vaults are often more easily entered through one of the walls, than through the securely locked door.

■ MACHINE GUN (15%)

Use this skill whenever firing bursts from a bipod or tripod mount. If single shots are fired from a bipod, use the Rifle skill instead if it is higher.

■ MARTIAL ARTS (00%)

Use when attacking with Fist/Punch, Head Butt, Kick, or Grapple. If the attack roll is equal to or less than the attacker's Martial Arts percentage, the attack does double damage. Thus Fist/Punch would do 2D3 plus normal damage bonus. Marital Arts doubles the damage done if the attack strikes home, but not any damage bonus.

A person with Martial Arts may choose which attack to parry just before that attack, and does not need to make a parry statement at the beginning of the round. Even with Martial Arts, bullets and other projectiles cannot be parried.

1920s Martial Arts

The only commonly known martial arts are the French *savat*, and Japanese Ju-Jutsu (or Jiu-Jitsu). The former is style of French kick boxing that includes Indo-Chinese features. The latter is traditional in Japan. More about it can be learned by reading K. Saito's book, *Jiu-Jitsu Tricks* (1905).

■ MECHANICAL REPAIR (20%)

This allows the investigator to repair a broken machine, or to create some new simple one. Basic carpentry and plumbing projects may be attempted. This is a companion skill to Electrical Repair, and both may be necessary to fix some devices. Special tools or parts may be required. Except for very simple locks, special tools are needed to pick locks. See the Locksmith skill.

1920s Mechanical Repair

A variety of mechanical chores abound today, from automobiles, to home appliances, to industry. Inexpensive correspondence courses and periodicals such as *Popular Mechanics* can keep a mechanic abreast of new developments.

In the 1920s basic electrical repair jobs can often be handled with Mechanical Repair (see Electrical Repair).

■ MEDICINE (05%)

The user diagnoses and treats human frailties, injuries, diseases, poisonings, etc., and makes public health recommendations. If an era has no good treatment for a malady, any effort is limited, uncertain, or inconclusive. Failure in application requires that the user wait some amount of time to try again, but another practitioner could make his or her attempt in the next round.

In an emergency, the successful user of Medicine can immediately restore 1D3 hit points, once per attack or injury.

In the same or the succeeding combat round, an investigator who has died may be returned to life if the emergency 1D3 hit points raises his or her hit point total to at least +1.

An investigator successfully treated with Medicine heals at 2D3 hit points per game week.

A success with Medicine immediately awakens any victim of a knock-out attack and, if the keeper wishes, anyone unconscious.

The keeper may rule that a medical condition is not treatable. See also First Aid.

1920s Medicine

The Great War results in X-ray machines that are fast and portable. Insulin is isolated in 1922. Sir Alexander Fleming discovers penicillin in 1928. By the end of the decade radiation therapy is being administered to cancer patients.

Nitrous Oxide is still the best general anaesthetic, despite tests with ethylene and acetylene. Cocaine is still the best topical anaesthetic, although quickly being replaced by synthetic Novocaine. Morphine, although regulated by the Federal Government, is the best massive pain-killer, and despite its addictive quality has still not completely lost its early "wonder drug" image. Antibiotics are non-existent and quinine is still used to treat such things as malaria and yellow fever. State-mandated vaccinations have nearly eliminated Small Pox as a threat and successes have been obtained against typhoid-type diseases. However, many others such as cholera and tuberculosis have proven resistant and remain virulent. A world-wide influenza epidemic in 1918-1919 infected twenty million in the U.S.A., resulting in 850,000 fatalities. It is estimated that the pandemic killed twenty million people, infecting every continent except Australia.

■ NATURAL HISTORY (10%)

Originally the study of plant and animal life in its environment. Even by the 1890s this study had long been divided into many separate academic disciplines. As a skill, it represents the knowledge of farmers, fishermen, inspired amateurs, and hobbyists. It identifies species and habits or milieu in a general way, and is able to guess at what is important to a particular species. What is known may or may not be accurate--this is the region of appreciation, tradition, and enthusiasm. Use Natural History to judge horseflesh at a county fair, or to decide whether a butterfly collection is excellent--or just excellently framed.

1920s Natural History

The first Okapi is bagged in Africa in 1900. The existence of the gorilla is confirmed in 1903 and two separate species identified. The creature is studied by American explorer Carl Akeley. On September 1, 1914, the last American Passenger Pigeon dies in a Cincinnati zoo.

■ NAVIGATE (10%)

Allows the user to find his or her way in storms, clear weather, in day, or at night. Those of higher skill are familiar with the astronomical tables, charts, and instruments. Rolled results for such a skill should be kept secret, a matter for the investigators to work out. One could also use this skill to measure and map an area--an island of many square miles, a passage, or the inside of a room.

■ OCCULT (05%)

This skill enables the user to recognize occult paraphernalia, words, and concepts, as well as identify grimoires of magic and occult codes when he sees them, and the skill can aid in their translation or understanding. Comprehending certain books may provide percentiles of Occult. Some occult books are noted in the Magic chapter. This skill does not apply to spell books, and magic of the Cthulhu Mythos, but as most of the more ignorant human worshipers of the Great Old Ones may believe in the conventional occult as well, it could prove of use.

1920s Occult

In 1920 Aleister Crowley founds the Abbey of Thelema in Sicily; he is expelled in 1923 after the death of one of the members. In 1925 Sir Arthur Conan Doyle is nominated honorary president of the International Spirit Congress. In the same year Col. Percy Fawcett disappears in the jungles of Brazil while searching for evidence of Atlantis. The mystic Gurdjieff sets up a little publicized institute near Paris.

Popular books of the era include: *The Encyclopedia of Occultism* (1920) by Lewis Spence; *The Witch-Cult of Western Europe* (1921) by Dr. Margaret Murray; *Thirty Years of Psychical Research* (1923) by Charles Richet; *The Problem of Atlantis* (1924) by Lewis Spence; The Old Straight Track (1925) by Alfred Watkins; The Lost Continent of Mu (1926) by Col. James Churchward; and *The Projection of the Astral Body* (1929) by Dr. Hereward Carrington.

■ OPERATE HEAVY MACHINERY (00%)

Required to drive and operate a tank, backhoe, steam shovel, or other large-scale construction machine. Once the skill is known, no skill roll is needed except for difficult or dangerous tasks, or bad or dangerous conditions. For very different sorts of machines, the keeper may decide to lower an investigator's nominal skill if the problems encountered are mostly unfamiliar ones: someone used to running a bulldozer, for instance, will not be fully competent with a steam turbine in a ship's engine room.

■ OTHER LANGUAGE (00%)

Specify the language. No limit exists on the number which an individual can know. The skill represents the user's chance to speak, read, and write in a language other than his or her own. Ancient or unknown languages comparable to Aklo should not be chosen, but ordinary earthly languages may be. Occasionally the keeper may determine that a number of separate complex points exist in a document or speech, and call for several such language rolls, one for each point. Similarly, the keeper may momentarily reduce a user's skill in a language if archaic speech or writing in that language is encountered. Normally a single successful Other Language roll is needed to comprehend an entire book.

If an investigator has points in a particular Other Language, he or she always grasps the gist of normal conversation, though one needs INT x5 or better points in a second language to pass for a native speaker. Blank spaces exist on the investigator sheet for other languages.

To identify an unknown present-day human language, use a History or Archaeology roll. To identify an alien language, use a Cthulhu Mythos or possibly an Occult roll.

1920s Other Language

Many modern languages are related. An investigator skilled in French could logically argue for a fairly accurate understanding of Spanish, Italian, or Portuguese. Keepers will have to adjudicate which languages are sufficiently related, and to what extent their relationship aids in understanding.

■ OWN LANGUAGE (EDU x5%)

Specify the language. In infancy and early childhood, most humans use a single language. For most people in the United States, that tongue is some dialect of American English. But whatever the tongue chosen by the player for the investigator's Own Language, the investigator's skill in Own Language automatically starts at EDU x5%: thereafter the investigator speaks, reads, and writes at that percentage or higher. Normally no skill roll is necessary to use Own Language. If a document is extremely difficult to read, or in an archaic dialect, the keeper may reduce the user's skill chance in that situation.

■ PERSUADE (15%)

Use Persuade to firmly convince a target of a particular idea or concept. Like Fast talk, Persuade may be employed without reference to truth. Unlike Fast Talk, Persuade's effect lingers indefinitely, for weeks or years perhaps, until events or another Persuade turn the target's mind in another direction. Since Persuade's effects are long-lasting, the successful application of the skill might take an hour or more, depending on what's being attempted.

■ PHARMACY (00%)

The user recognizes, compounds, and dispenses a wide variety of drugs and potions, natural and man-made, and understands side-effects and contraindications. He or she has a good knowledge of poisons and antidotes. The skill grants no ability to diagnose diseases or to prescribe medicines, though the user may be familiar with a range of symptoms and be able to select the right treatments for poisonings.

1920s Pharmacy

Salvarsan was discovered in 1910, the first effective treatment for syphilis. Various dyes and compounds have been found to 'flush' the human system of parasitical protozoa but stubborn bacteria still pose a problem. The nutritional role of newly-discovered vitamins is being studied. Experiments are being conducted with certain "hypnotic" drugs--various alkaloids isolated from exotic plants.

The Federal Food and Drug Act of 1906 imposed strict requirements on the contents and labeling of patent medicines and other nostrums, resulting in the general demise of this industry. The Harrison Anti-Narcotic Act further strictly controls the dispensing of drugs such as morphine, cocaine, and others.

■ PHOTOGRAPHY (10%)

Covers both still and motion photography. This skill allows one to take clear pictures, develop them properly, and perhaps enhance half-hidden detail. Failures are blurred or do not show what was desired.

1920s Photography

Coin-operated photo machines debut on the boardwalks, delivering four different photographs for ten cents. T. Svedberg is using ultra-violet light to photograph ancient documents, allowing for the deciphering of palimpsests, and for the discovery of forgeries as well. Cameras have been developed that photograph the inside of gun barrels, and through microscopes. Long exposure photographs reveal otherwise invisible stars and nebulae. Continuing research promises newer, faster, and more sensitive film emulsions all the time.

■ PHYSICS (00%)

Grants theoretical understanding of pressure, materials, motion, magnetism, electricity, optics, radioactivity and related phenomena, and some ability to construct experimental devices to test ideas. The degree of knowledge depends on the era of use. Practical devices such as automobiles are not the province of physicists, but impractical or experimental devices may be, perhaps in conjunction with Electronics or Mechanical Repair.

1920s Physics

Albert Einstein's theories of relativity (1905 and 1916), Max Planck's quantum mechanics, Neils Bohr's model of the atom, and the Heisenberg Uncertainly Principle (1927) all point to a new, and possibly terrifying understanding of our universe.

■ PILOT (00%)

The air/water equivalent of Drive Automobile, this is the maneuver skill for flying or floating craft. An investigator might have several versions of this skill in the spaces on the investigator sheet, each starting at 00%. Without believable personal history explaining, for example, otherwise, the skill should be taken as relating only to craft of modest size.

Pilot Aircraft skills change from era to era. Pilot Boat does not change, and does not distinguish between sail and motor craft. The same sorts of modifying conditions--bad weather, bad visibility, or damage--apply to air and water craft.

A skill user with 1 or more point of skill can start and then set sail or take off on a calm day with good visibility. Require Pilot rolls for storms, navigation, by instruments, low visibility, and other difficult situations.

PILOT BOAT: understands the behavior of small motor and sailing craft in wind, storms, and tides, and can read wave and wind action to suggest hidden obstacles and approaching storms. Novice sailors may find difficult the mere docking of a rowboat.

PILOT AIRCRAFT: understands and is increasingly competent with a general class of aircraft, as summarized below. Upon any landing, even under the best conditions, a Pilot roll must be made. If conditions are good, double the chance for success. If conditions are bad, the pilot lands at his or her normal chance. Ordinarily, a failure represents only some sort of damage to the craft, which must be repaired before the next takeoff, but pilot and passengers walk away with minor injury. A result of 00 is a memorable disaster, with at least one death.

Each class of aircraft counts as a different skill, and should be listed independently, or as the keeper sees fit. The 1920s could include such possibilities as balloons, dirigibles, prop-powered aircraft, and gliders.

1920s Air Pilots

Famous German dirigible pilot Hugo Eckener crosses the Atlantic (1924), travels around the world (1929), and makes a trans-polar flight (1931). Eddie Rickenbacker, America's World War Ace, currently employed at Cadillac, joins American Airways in 1932. Charles Lindbergh makes his famous crossing of the Atlantic in 1927 and returns to a ticker-tape parade in New York City.

■ PSYCHOANALYSIS (00%)

Enables the user to staunch temporary and indefinite insanity for a day or so. If the condition persists beyond that period, thereafter the unfortunate lapses, and only time heals the insanity. This emergency treatment takes up to an hour to perform, and can be applied just once per incident of insanity, no matter how many analysts are available.

Treatment by a psychotherapist can add Sanity points during indefinite insanity and possibly speed recovery. See the Sanity chapter.

Psychoanalysis cannot increase a person's Sanity points beyond POW x5, nor above 99-Cthulhu Mythos.

The skill refers to the range of emotional therapies, not just to Freudian procedures. Formal psychotherapy was little-known in the 1890s, though some procedures are as old as humanity. Often it was looked on as suspect charlatanry in the 1920s. The common term then for an analyst or scholar of emotional disorders was 'alienist.'

1920s Psychoanalysis

Europe leads the U.S. in this field. The first public clinic and training school opens in Berlin in 1921, followed shortly by a similar facility in Vienna. The single major journal available in English is *The International Journal of Psycho-Analysis*.

Although Sigmund Freud is still the recognized authority, writing *A General Introduction to Psychoanalysis* (1915-1916), and *The Ego and the Id* (1923), many of his students and colleagues have broken with him, devising their own theories. Otto Rank develops the concept of 'birth-anxiety' and publishes *The Myth of the Birth of the Hero* (1909), and *The Trauma of Birth* (1924). Alfred Adler talks about the 'will to power' in *Understanding Human Nature* (1918). Carl Jung describes a 'will to life' and postulates the existence of the collective unconscious with *Psychology of the Unconscious* (1916), and *Psychological Types* (1923).

■ PSYCHOLOGY (05%)

A skill common to all humans, it allows the user to study an individual and form an idea of his or her motives and character. In general, the keeper should make the rolls for this skill and keep the results secret, announcing only the information, true or false, that the user gained by employing it. Players should not expect that this skill penetrates skillful deceit unless the investigators jar their opponent's confidence.

1920s Psychology

Although natural psychology has long been employed by shamans, healers, fortune-tellers, and con-men, it is only since the mid-19th century, as a branch of philosophy, that it has been the subject of study by academics. In Europe Karl Marbe studies 'awareness,' and Henry Watt 'thinking.' Narziss Ach studies 'systematic experimental introspection,' and Karl Buhler 'imageless thought.' Koffka and Kohler lay the foundations of 'gestalt,' and Le Bon and Sighele study 'suggestion' and 'mob psychology.' In America Simon and Binet develop the first IQ tests in 1908, and Watson launches the concept of 'behaviorism' in 1913. Catell forms the Psychological Corporation in 1921 to promote the use of psychology in industry. Meanwhile, in the Soviet Union, Stalin initiates investigations into ESP, telekinesis, and other paranormal events. Duke University, in the U.S.A., follows the Russian lead in the early 1930s.

The current leading publication is *The American Journal of Psychology*, founded 1887.

■ RIDE (05%)

Intended to apply to saddle horses, donkeys, or mules on easy terrain. A camel might be ridden successfully at a lowered percentage chance. The skill also grants knowledge of basic care of the riding animal, riding gear, and how to handle the steed at the gallop.

Should a steed do something unexpected, such as rearing, then the investigator's chance of remaining seated equals his or her Ride. If an investigator falls from a mount, either because the animal has collapsed, fallen, or died, or because a Ride roll failed, he or she loses 1D6 hit point in the accident. A successful Jump roll saves 1D6 hit points.

Wielding a weapon effectively while riding takes both a weapon skill and a Ride in excess of 50%, and the keeper might apply modifiers to reflect the situation.

1920s Ride

Although riding horses, camels, or elephants requires individual skills, there is enough similarity that an investigator's beginning skill with a new type of mount should never be less than half his best Ride skill.

■ RIFLE (25%)

Permits the user to fire any type of rifle, whether lever-action, bolt-action, or semi-automatic. When a military-style assault rifle is used n the 1990s to fire a burst, use this skill. When a shotgun fires a rifled slug, use this skill.

At the keeper's option, combine Rifle and Shotgun as a single skill differentiating only between pellet and slug ammunition.

■ SHOTGUN (30%)

With this skill any scatter-gun can be fired. Since the load expands in a spreading pattern, the user's chance to hit does not decrease with range, but the damage done does. At ranges from 10-20 yards, 1D3 close-together targets can be hit with one round, and from 20-50 yards, 1D6 targets can be hit. The keeper decides whether the targets are close enough for this rule.

Double-barreled shotguns can be sawn off, for purposes of concealment. See the firearms tables for data. In the United States, such weapons become illegal in the 1920s (1934--federal law).

If firing a rifled slug, use the Rifle skill. At the keeper's option, combine Rifle and Shotgun as a single skill, differentiating only between pellet and slug ammo.

■ SNEAK (10%)

The art of moving quietly, without alerting those who might hear. Used in combination with Hide, the investigator makes a single D100 roll, the result of which is matched against the investigator's percentages in both skills. Use this combination when silent movement is necessary. See also Hide.

1920s Sneak

Quiet shoes with gum soles can add bonus of 10-20 points.

■ SPOT HIDDEN (25%)

This skill allows the user to spot a secret door or compartment, hidden intruder, inconspicuous clue, interesting piece of evidence, concealed car, ambushers, or anything similar. One of the more important skills in the game, with a straightforward application.

1920s Spot Hidden

Binoculars, telescopes, and game finders may all add to Spot Hidden.

■ SUBMACHINE GUN (15%)

When firing any submachine gun, use this skill.

■ SWIM (25%)

The ability to stay afloat and moving in water or other liquid. Immersed, use a Swim roll to keep from drowning or to move through the medium. A failing Swim roll starts the drowning procedure. Someone drowning may receive a Swim roll attempt each round--with a success, he or she reaches the surface and breathes. With a second success, he or she can begin to move through the water. If the second Swim roll fails, drowning begins again.

Inflatable water wings can be purchased for 35 cents.

1920s Swim

World records in the late 1920s are: 100 Yards, 51 seconds (Johnny Weismuller); Mile Swim, 21 minutes, 6 1/4 seconds; The English Channel, 11 hours, 5 minutes.

■ THROW (25%)

To hit a target with a casual object, or to hit a target with the right part of the object thrown (such as the blade of a knife or hatchet), use Throw. A palm-sized object of reasonable balance can be hurled three yards for each STR point of the investigator which exceeds the object's SIZ. However, an object designed to be thrown can be hurled up to six yards for each STR point in excess of the object's SIZ, and perhaps bounce on for more. Keepers must choose the multiplier suitable to the actual object since, for instance, a baseball behaves differently than a javelin.

If the throw roll fails, then randomly determine where the object lands, using the closeness of the actual die roll result to the desired result to indicate nearness.

1920s Throw

World records in the late 1920s are: discus, 157 feet, 1 5/8 inches; javelin 222 feet, 9 inches; Shotput (16 lbs.), 52 feet, 1/16 inch.

■ TRACK (10%)

With Track, an investigator can follow a person, vehicle, or animal over soft earth and leaves. Subtract 10% from the chance for success for each day that passes since the tracks were made. Rain may make tracking impossible. A being cannot be tracked across water, over concrete, or at night except in unusual circumstances.

1920s Track

This skill extends to other tracks, such as auto tires. Plaster casts can be made, and used for later comparison with suspects.

Five New Skills

■ BLOCK (DEX x2%)

A highly recommended optional skill, Block allows a character to use large objects for defense. Barstools, shotguns, lengths of pipe, a tree branch--anything that can be held up with two hands to intercept a blow may be used in conjunction with the Block skill. Successful use means the object intercepted the blow, although it should be noted that if damage exceeds the hit points of the item, it either breaks or is knocked loose and the remaining damage points inflicted on the character.

Like the Dodge skill, beginning skill is DEX x2, and may increase with successful use. It does not replace Parry skills used in conjunction with weapons designed for parrying, such as swords.

■ ROPING (00%)

This is the ability to twirl and throw a rope, lassoing a target. It is a skill most common to cowboys and mountain climbers and requires a well-worked rope for normal chances of success. A fresh, stiff rope from the store reduces the chances of success by as much as one half.

A thrown rope has a maximum range of STR x1 yard, if thrown laterally across the ground. Trying to throw a loop of rope vertically, trying to loop an overhead object, reduces the range by one half.

■ DISGUISE (00%)

This is the skill of using makeup, wigs, costumes, and other devices to alter one's appearance. Disguise can be used to make a person appear as someone else, even of a different race or sex. Injuries, scars, and other disfigurements can also be simulated.

Note that this skill only allows appearances to be altered. A knowledge of background, class values, or other details may be necessary to fully pull off a disguise. Actually impersonating a known person requires acting talent, voice control, and a good deal of luck.

■ FORENSICS (00%)

This skill represents the investigators working knowledge of current scientific detective skills. It includes such things as: the ability to properly collect and compare fingerprints; how to make ballistics checks; the value of blood samples; and numerous other techniques. See Appendix B: 1920s Forensics for further details.

■ HYPNOTISM (00%)

To successfully hypnotize someone, the subject must be willing to undergo the treatment. If the hypnotist fails his roll, he is unable to hypnotize that character until his skill is somehow increased, at which time he may attempt it again. If the roll is successful, the subject is now hypnotized and can be hypnotized in the future by this same investigator automatically, without the necessity of making a roll.

Hypnosis can be used in several ways.

AID TO PSYCHOANALYSIS: If an investigator can successfully hypnotize a subject, the investigator may add 25 percentiles to his current Psychoanalysis score (provided he has 10 or more points to begin with) when treating this patient.

POST-HYPNOTIC SUGGESTION: A subject can be implanted with a suggestion to perform a single specific action in response to a key word or event. Note that it is impossible to implant a suggestion that goes against the subject's basic nature. While a person can usually be made to do something foolish in public, they will not attack and try to kill someone--unless that is part of their normal behavior pattern.

MEMORY AID: Often characters go insane upon witnessing some key event and suffer amnesia, forgetting about what may have taken place. Successful use of hypnosis can dredge up these buried memories.

The Professional Investigator

Pro Tips, The Art of Investigation, Witness Psychology.

THE ONE THING THAT separates the professional private investigator from the amateur is that photostatic copy of his license, ready to be presented when proof of profession is demanded. With it comes legality, legitimacy, and professionalism. In the same way that police build their case, so can the private detective. If a client has hired you to find out if her husband is cheating on her, you can take those incriminating photographs without risking an invasion of privacy charge. If the client signed the contract, and is paying you her hard-earned money, those photographs are legal. If the nosy reporter tries this number he gets hit with a libel suit, and probably loses. A private investigator can question people at liberty, and they can no more be accused of harassment than can the police.

Everything a professional investigator does with regards to your client and his case, as long as it conforms to the ethics of the profession, is legal. No one has to talk to a private investigator, but then, nobody has to talk to the police, either. The police are *public* investigators, the hired detective a *private* investigator.

Ethics are important; a private investigator lives and dies by them. If he breaks and enters, even in the name of a client, he has committed an illegal act and, if caught, will have his license pulled so fast his head won't stop spinning until there's a Democrat in office again--to say nothing of possible jail time. But the code of ethics is a shield, as well. A privileged relationship exists between investigator and client that allows the investigator to maintain private any information gathered in the name of his client. Though the local police may not like it, unless they can prove you're withholding evidence vital to an investigation, they can't do much about it. Professional ethics cut both ways.

Obtaining a License

Without a license you cannot legally advertise yourself, or in any way represent yourself as a private detective. Licensing is a function of individual states, each with different requirements and different ethical standards by which an investigator is judged. Basic requirements, however, are much the same.

All applicants must provide proof of investigative experience. Generally this can be ten years with a police department, five years as an insurance or other professional investigator, or a lengthy apprenticeship with another licensed detective or agency. The actual amount of experience required differs from state to state but three years minimum is a safe bet. This experience shows that the applicant not only knows how to conduct a proper investigation, but that the applicant also understands the legal ramifications of the profession. Letters of recommendation may also be required, and a signed affidavit may be needed as well, providing proof of the experience.

Next, an applicant has to post a bond with a recognized bondsman, probably a minimum of $500. This is the private investigator's legal collateral, his insurance if sued, and part of his credit rating. An applicant must be able to show that they are not a financial risk. Some states require a private investigator to have an established place of business before the license is issued. An office with an address, and perhaps a working telephone, is usually required. This is the state's insurance--the board does not want to license fly-by-night outfits.

Then there's the background check. The applicant must demonstrate good mental health, and a relatively clean record. Convicted murderers or extortionists are unlikely to pass. Relatives and friends may be contacted and questioned by state investigators, and the applicant's finances probably examined as well.

Finally, an applicant must pass a written exam, and, in some states, an oral exam as well. This determines general ability, intelligence, and knowledge, as well as revealing the applicant's familiarity with the law and investigative techniques. In most states an applicant may take the exam as many times as needed until a passing grade is finally achieved, but the fee must be paid each time. Once acquired, the license will have to be renewed periodically, but this is a simpler process. However, the license can be suspended or revoked any time the licensing board feels that the detective is not performing up to standards.

A valid Private Detective's license does not impart the right to carry weapons. Concealed weapon permits are a separate matter, and may take as long as six months to obtain, possibly involving a second background check. When applying for a 'carry' permit, the applicant must present sufficient reason for carrying a firearm, and although being a private investigator is a good reason, it doesn't guarantee the permit will be issued.

Pro Tip–Basics

Every workman needs his tools and the private investigator is no different. Most of ours, however, are used for one thing: information gathering.

Primary tools are your contacts--the people you know. They define just how good an investigator you are--so get lots of them. These are the people to turn to for advice, information, and expertise: doctors, lawyers, bartenders, cabbies, garbage men (always check a suspect's garbage), and librarians as well. Clerks at city hall or the police department are even better. Someone high up in the city's bureaucracy is best. The police are not your enemy, so get to know a few, especially the local desk sergeant. Share a little information with them and they might share some with you. By the same token, criminal contacts are important in case you tread on the wrong toes. Never offend the mob, because they don't forget.

Your first recourse and most powerful weapon is the telephone. Not everybody has one, but every private eye should. You need a copy of the phone book and a working relationship with the local exchange operators. And, incidentally, start your firm's name with the letter 'A.' Most people call the first name they see in the book.

With a few calls you can find most things. But private eyes are not hired to find 'most things' so you'll need a comfortable pair of shoes for when you need to ask around; you will do a lot of walking. You can get into virtually anywhere if you look like you belong, so acquire a varied wardrobe. Simple, smart suits are best, and trench coats useful for their big pockets--but workman's clothes are handy too. Interviewing working-class people doesn't mean dressing down though; a look of authority doesn't hurt a bit.

If anyone ever gives you a business card, keep it; salesmen's are best. False identification is always useful. You will also need cigarettes because they make good bribes and ice-breakers, and are an excuse to carry a light--invaluable for disposing of evidence.

Speaking of bribes, remember that most things run smoother if appreciation is shown for services rendered. Some people get antsy at the notion of anything resembling a bribe, so keep in mind that goods, services, and information are handy alternatives to cash.

The Investigator and The Law

If an investigation has any contact with a police investigation there may be friction--especially if your client is a suspect, or if the police have reason to believe the private eye is withholding evidence. By law, evidence pertinent to a police investigation must be turned over immediately. The client-investigator relationship does not permit the investigator to avoid this responsibility. For the most part police leave private investigators alone, and a wise private eye does the same. A private investigator encountering something clearly illegal--a crime in progress--is as obliged as the next citizen to report it to the police. However, a private investigator's license does not require a detective to get involved with crimes outside the sphere of his own investigations. There is no requirement they fight crime at every turn. However, like any citizen, a private investigator witnessing a felony is free to perform a citizen's arrest.

As a licensed business, a private investigator is required to file tax returns and provide insurance and benefits for his employees. As a consequence many private investigators sub-contract to other agencies to avoid the problems of adding agents to their own payrolls. A private detective should write a contract for every case assumed, describing the parameters of the job, as well as the fee to be paid. Such contracts may include waivers of negligence and/or malpractice.

Pro Tip–Firearms

You may not want to use a gun but I do, more for its persuasive effect than killing power. That's why I like the .32. It's light, and I'd rather get off a lot of shots quickly and be sure of winging someone, than a single shot that either blows the victim's head off or misses completely. Three points to bear in mind: 1) Never think that you have to draw a gun to intimidate someone; 2) Never draw a gun unless someone is threatening violence; 3) If you start shooting at someone, expect them to shoot back.

Basically, avoid gunfights. If you need to hurt someone it is much better to rely on a right hook; it is less likely to kill, and the police get touchy about murder. Worse still, the science of forensic ballistics is currently more advanced in the U.S. (and New York in particular) than anywhere else in the world. A weapon used in a crime can often be traced directly back to its owner--and the prime suspect.

The Art of Investigation

THE FIRST PRIORITY in investigating a crime is to determine that a crime has, in fact, been committed. That robbery may just be a misplaced wallet. That decapitated body may have been an unfortunate auto accident. Then again, if that decapitated body is also showing signs of a struggle--say, blood and hair underneath its fingernails--it's probably a safe bet that this was a murder. We now have a crime, and the following rules are in effect.

Securing the Crime Scene

First, the crime scene must be secured. This means that nobody touches anything until the appropriate authorities arrive. All people at the scene should be detained until they have been as least cursorily questioned, the simple premise being that the last person on the scene is the most likely perpetrator. Nothing at the crime scene should be touched or altered in any way until the reigning authority gives the all clear. This authority may be anyone from the local beat cop to the Chief Medical Examiner and his entourage, depending on the situation.

Detaining Witnesses

Second, witnesses must be sought and held until they've given a statement. This can be a lot more trouble than it's worth, but you never know who heard what or saw what, and witnesses are the cornerstone of any legal case. But witnesses are a tricky business; you never know if they have a bone to pick with a next-door neighbor and are giving false testimony.

Police tend to grab any suspicious looking person found at a crime scene send them downtown. Private detectives cannot do this, of course, but they can request names and addresses, with the intention of questioning these individuals later.

Contacting Authorities

Third, the appropriate professionals are called. The police, the coroner's office, and so on. In the case of a murder, nobody touches anything until the primary detective arrives. Photographs are taken whenever possible, and detectives make their own sketches of the crime scene in their notebooks.

Examining the Scene

Everything is examined. Some investigators walk through the entire house or apartment before viewing the actual scene itself, trying to reconstruct the victim's life. What's in the kitchen? If it's lunchtime and the trash can is full of fresh orange peels you have an idea what might have been eaten for lunch. Remember to ask about that at the autopsy--see if the orange was in the victim's stomach.

What doors and windows are open? Have any of the locks been forced or picked? It's nearly impossible to pick a lock without leaving some evidence. Nothing was forced? Is this a bad part of town? If so, the doors should

Pro Tip–Remembering People

The oldest system of remembering people is known as a portrait parlé (word-picture), which describes an individual's physical characteristics. It is still an effective method if used discreetly. The technique involves categorizing the elements of the face and body. Not just the obvious sex, eyes, hair, height and weight, but also the shape of the nose, lips, brow, hands, and so on. Also note any marks incurred by profession such as ink stains, scars, or callouses.

Listen to the subject's voice for any peculiar inflections or unusual phrases. When they tell you their name remember it and write it down later, along with a brief portrait parlé. Look them in the eye when you speak. Unless they're a salesman, they probably glance away giving you an opportunity to look them over. See how they move; comportment and clothes, especially shoes, are a good indication of wealth and therefore social class--a handy thing to know when talking to them.

Pro Tip–Interviews

Always develop a list of questions beforehand. There is nothing more embarrassing than deciding to go and see a witness and then ending up doing nothing but staring at them after you've asked only one or two questions. Whenever possible research your subject first, and be ready to follow up on the answers they give to your first questions. The more important they are to your enquiries, the more background work you need to do. If they are a witness to a crime, take a look at the crime scene first, then find out what you can about the witness from libraries, public records, or newspaper archives--even their laundry bags or trash cans. Talk to people who know the subject--co-workers, paperboys, neighbors, and others. Find out about their social class, home life, interests, and attitudes. People are more likely to reveal information about someone they know if they think that they are helping that person. Learn to be discreet.

Keep statements short and to the point. People respond to quick demands without thinking. Throw someone a smoking gun and shout: "Hold this!" and nine times out of ten they will. Be sure of what you say. Before blurting out something hard to swallow, put yourself in their shoes and think how you would react to what you are about to ask.

If you want something from someone, don't let them think that that is all you're interested in. They have problems of their own and while their problems aren't as important as yours, make it seem like you think they are. Ask how they are, share a quick joke and get them into the habit of agreeing with you. Try not to phrase your questions so they require negative answers. Keep nodding--it makes them nod too. Salesmen call this the 'yes' mode.

Private Eye: "Hard day?"
Clerk: "Yeah."
Private Eye: "Boss overworks you, huh?"
Clerk: "You bet."
Private Eye: "Say, could you do me a quick favor?"
Clerk: "Sure."

have been locked, right? So, we know the perpetrator may have been let in, rather than having to force his way in. Maybe they had a key, or knew someone in the family. What's missing? A shoe in the closet that doesn't have a mate? A mug of shaving soap but no razor to be found?

And nothing should be touched. Fingerprints need to be taken. Although it is only rarely that a usable print is found and then matched--say 10% of the time, at best--it's still a 10% bonus above and beyond any other possibilities.

The crime is reconstructed at the scene to the best of the investigator's ability. A dead body with the back of its head missing and a .45 at its feet might be a suicide, or maybe a murder. If there are powder burns around the mouth and on the victim's hand, and if the exit trajectory is up instead of down--the blood spatters following the exit of the wound--it's probably safe to call it a suicide. But run the gun for prints--and see if you can find the bullet, just in case a ballistics check ends up being called for.

Physical evidence is vital to any case: cigarette ash on the carpet but the owner doesn't smoke; a footprint outside the window that can be cast in plaster, maybe the shoe identified. Depth of impression, and length of stride if you find a pair of prints, can give an idea of how tall and heavy the perpetrator is. The means of entry is physical evidence too. Was the door forced, the window broken, or did the perpetrator talk their way in? All of this is the M.O., or *modus operandi*, and remember, the police keep records. If Jerry the Slick used to like to kick in doors and then break all the windows in a place, maybe it was Jerry the Slick who kicked in this door and broke all the windows in this place.

Phone records are also considered physical evidence and should never be overlooked. Who the victim recently talked to may lead to learning who committed the crime. Operators are usually more than willing to assist police or detectives solve a crime.

Witness Psychology

Most people don't like to lie, and it shows. It is a subconscious thing that can be suppressed actively for a while, but eventually the guard always drops and they start showing 'lie-signs.' I can tell when someone is lying to me by the sweat on their top lip, hands, and forehead. People often start to fidget when forced to lie for extended periods of time: folding their arms, touching their nose or ears, tapping their feet, fiddling with their fingers, or looking around in an apparently disinterested fashion. Their voice may rise in pitch. They might start denying heavily ("I swear! I had nothing to do with it!"), or challenge you ("What's it got to do with you?"), or simply avoid the point ("I don't have the faintest idea of what you're talking about.") Innocent people almost always talk at great length when accused of something--despite

Last Tip--Operating Above and Beyond the Law

There is only so much one can learn through standard avenues of enquiry. At some point breaking the law may be essential to gaining the information you want. I don't mean some minor infraction of a city ordinance, I mean actually committing a felony.

The most common crime investigators commit is breaking and entering. When all else fails, you can rely on a good crowbar to get you the facts the deepest conspiracies seek to conceal. Obviously I can't commit everything to writing, but remember--always wear gloves!

Successfully committing a crime is a matter of minimizing risks. First, consider if the action is necessary. Crime should never be your first resort, always your last. Habitually breaking the law is bad--there is no sense taking any unnecessary risks in this profession.

If you must do it, then pick your time and place carefully. Essentially, if no one discovers that a crime has been committed, then it wasn't. The best location to perform the more unsavory crimes is far away from the prying eyes and ears of civilization. However, most situations call for the crime to be committed wherever the information is, such as an office. Remember what I said about getting into places simply by walking in and acting confident. Use this approach whenever possible.

If you have someone that is doing things illegal, it is difficult for them to bring the law down on you. If you steal from a gun-smuggler, they usually can't run to the cops. This is fine as far as it goes, but remember what I said before about the mob.

Crimes are best executed quickly so they are usually solo affairs. However, a lookout is a valuable asset if you know someone you can trust with your life. Choose your accomplices carefully.

Crime is a fact of life so don't worry too much about it. It's all part of the job.

their Fifth Amendment rights. They are normally eager to speak volumes, and dwell on facts rather than denials.

Oh, and by the way, although electric "lie detectors" have proven themselves useful, the evidence gained by them is not admissable in court.

In Conclusion

The great mystery is not so much in the crime itself, but in its solution. An investigator must train himself to ask questions about everything he sees. And he must ask the right questions. Why wasn't the door locked? Where did the checkbook go? What would I do if...? Each question gives a separate answer, and each answer brings the investigation closer to its conclusion, the resolution of the final question, the answer to the mystery.

Wrapping Up

One last thing: NEVER get emotionally involved in a case. As soon as you feel compassion for the sob stories you get handed--as genuine as they might be--you lose control of the case. It could even cost you your life. Remember it's just a job and people get hurt all the time--the other guy's problems don't amount to a hill of beans. ■

1920s Forensic Arts

Fingerprints, Forensic Ballistics, Blood Typing, Time of Death, The Autopsy, Other Forensic Developments.

MANY DEVELOPMENTS HAVE been made in the forensic sciences since the turn of the century. A brief overview of the current state of the art follows.

Fingerprints

Although fingerprints were first discovered to be unique in the late 18th century, actual proof, and the idea that they could be used to identify criminals, did not come about until the late 19th century. The first official fingerprint department was set up by the Central Police Department in La Plata, Argentina, in 1891. In 1901, London's New Scotland Yard created their own fingerprint bureau, soon after copied by other agencies. The ability of fingerprints to identify a suspect was acknowledged in the U.S. in 1903 when the outmoded Bertillon method (a system of gross physical measurements) confused the identification of a convicted criminal sent to Leavenworth Federal Prison. Only by fingerprinting were authorities able to sort the matter out.

In 1904 inspectors from Scotland Yard visited the States to teach the science of fingerprinting, resulting in its adoption by the U.S. military in 1908. By the 1920s, although several different classification systems are in use, the concept of fingerprints as a positive method of identification has been almost universally adopted by agencies around the world.

Criminal fingerprint files can be found in most state and local police agencies although their relative completeness, filing system, and general condition reflects local budgets and the concerns of personnel. Not until the late 1920s does the U.S. Bureau of Investigation begin compiling its vast fingerprint files, creating the first national fingerprint records in the country.

Forensic Ballistics

Charles E. Waite, of the New York State Prosecutor's Office, was the first person to collate ballistic data, analyzing guns from both home and abroad. His studies made it possible to use slugs and spent cartridges to identify the particular gun from which a bullet was fired. By 1922 Waite's work resulted in the formation of the New York Bureau of Forensic Ballistics. Here Phillip Gravelle adapted the comparison microscope to ballistic use while John Fisher invented the helixometer used to closely examine the interior of gun barrels.

Accurate identification depends on the condition of the slug retrieved. Usually the caliber can be determined by size and weight. Even the specific make of gun might be identified, using the pattern of microscopic grooves left on the slug by the rifling of the pistol or rifle. But some slugs are so damaged that even accurate identification of caliber is difficult.

Spent shells provide the most accurate way of identifying a weapon. Minute marks and scratches left by firing pins and ejection mechanisms can be matched to those made on shells test-fired from the weapon and the two compared. Note that shotgun slugs or pellets bare no specific marks. However, shotgun casings may bear marks from the weapon's firing and ejection mechanisms, allowing for a possible match.

In the case of a shooting death, the distance from which the weapon was fired can often be gauged by evidence found near the wound, sometimes an aid in determining whether a death was suicide or murder. A star-shaped burst in the skin around the wound indicates the muzzle was held directly against the body when fired. Soot smudges, easily wiped away, are usually found when the weapon was discharged less than twelve inches from the victim. At longer distances, sometimes up to three feet, the skin is 'tattooed' by small powder burns that do not wash or wipe away.

Blood Typing

Reliable tests to distinguish human blood from animal blood have been around since the late 19th century. Although in 1901 Karl Landsteiner discovered four major blood types, naming them A,B,O, and AB, blood typing was not used as a law enforcement tool until 1923 when the Italian, Latte, discovered an easy method for checking blood type using only the smallest of samples. After using his method to solve a couple baffling cases, a conference held in West Germany in 1926 publicly recognized the usefulness of Latte's methods.

By 1925 Japanese researchers are discovering that a large percentage of the population are "secretors," people whose blood type can be determined from samples of other bodily secretions including saliva and semen. A Japanese murder is solved in 1928 using this knowledge. It should be noted that secretion samples must be reasonably fresh to produce reliable results.

In America, it is 1934 before the first major police chemical and toxicological laboratory is established in New York, and 1938 before the first serological laboratory equipped to study bloodstains in the manner pioneered by European criminologists.

Still of limited use are the thousands of blood spatter samples created by the Frenchmen, Florence and Fricon. These cards show examples of blood that has been dripped, splattered, sprayed by artery, or thrown by different sorts of weapons.

Time of Death and the Autopsy

How long has someone been dead? Although rates vary according to temperature and other factors, the following can be used as a rough guideline.

Thirty minutes after death the skin becomes purplish, taking on a waxy look while lips and nails turn pale. Blood begins to settle in the lower parts of the body. Extremities turn blue, and eyeballs flatten as fluid pressure drops.

Rigor mortis begins to set in about four hours after death, beginning with the smallest muscles, spreading to the larger. It disappears in the same manner, and after thirty hours all traces of rigor are usually gone.

By the time twenty-fours has passed, the body has cooled to the temperature of its environment. Discoloration begins, the head and neck turning a greenish-red that spreads through the rest of the corpse over the next few days. Decomposition sets in, features become unrecognizable, and the odor of rotting meat is noticeable.

Three days later the corpse bloats, and gas blisters may form on the surface of the skin. Body fluids leak from orifices.

After three weeks, nails separate and fall out. The skin bursts open, revealing muscles and fat. In warm temperatures the body is reduced to a skeleton in three to four weeks, longer in colder temperatures.

The Autopsy

A full autopsy includes: identification and tagging of the body; measuring and weighing; an external examination noting all wounds and other marks; dissection and examination of the internal organs; toxicological examination of body fluids and organs, and examination of the stomach's contents; an opinion is rendered and a 'cause of death' noted on the death certificate.

Other Forensic Developments

In 1908 an English murderer is convicted on the basis of soil samples taken from his shoes and matched to soil from the murder scene. A report on the investigation, outlining methods of soil identification, is published in 1918.

A 1909 murder in Paris leads to the first conviction of a criminal based partially on the matching of human hairs. Again in France, in 1912, a murderer confesses to a crime when presented with evidence of his involvement gained from examining the dust on his clothing. In Berkeley, California, a vacuum cleaner is being used to accumulate microscopic evidence before 1920.

Dental records are occasionally used to verify the identity of a corpse. X-rays are found to be blocked by the metals in modern inks, helping identify forgeries. Ultraviolet light reveals erasures and other alterations to documents. ■

Chaosium Inc.
SELECTED TITLES

SINCE 1974

FICTION

THE HASTUR CYCLE

#6001 **$9.95**

Cthulhu Mythos stories by the original authors.

ISBN 1-56882-009-7

MYSTERIES OF THE WORM

#6002 **$9.95**

A collection of Lovecraftian tales written by master storyteller Robert Bloch.

ISBN 1-56882-012-7

CTHULHU'S HEIRS

#6003 **$9.95**

New Cthulhu Mythos fiction! This trade paperback contains 19 original stories and 2 rare reprints focusing on the Cthulhu Mythos and the mosnters, denizens, worshipers, and victims thereof.

ISBN 1-56882-013-5

CASTLE OF EYES

#6000 **$14.95**

A woman wakes from pain-filled dreams to find herself trapped in the Castle of Eyes.

ISBN 1-56882-005-4

KING OF SARTAR

#4500 **$14.95**

The facts, history, and secrets of Prince Argrath's heroic struggle against the invading Lunar Empire.

ISBN 0-933635-99-0

NEW CARD GAME

CREDO! The Game of Dueling Dogmas

#1011 **$14.95**

A new card game combining hilarity with history for two or more players. Players represent factions of the early Christian church, competing for flock and striving to have your doctrines accepted as the belief of the one Church.

ISBN 1-56882-008-9

ELRIC!

ELRIC! is a new heroic, swords & sorcery roleplaying game based on the fantasy novels of noted British author Michael Moorcock.

ELRIC!

#2900 **$19.95**

Everything that you need to play including rules, character-creation instructions, hints, tips, and adventures.

ISBN 0-933635-98-2

MELNIBONÉ

#2901 **$20.95**

Background, new magic, and adventures.

ISBN 1-56882-001-1

THE ELRIC GAMEMASTER SCREEN

#2902 **$14.95**

Summaries of important rules, spells, tables, and special options for combat.

ISBN 1-56882-011-9

ADVENTURES COMPATIBLE WITH ELRIC!

ROGUE MISTRESS

#2111 **$18.95**

A high-powered, dangerous campaign aboard a dimension-traveling ship.

ISBN 0-933635-73-7

SORCERERS OF PAN TANG

#2112 **$18.95**

Evil bad-guys and chief rivals of the Melnibonéans.

ISBN 0-933635-79-6

PERILS OF THE YOUNG KINGDOMS

#2113 **$18.95**

Five adventures exploring marvelous, mysterious, and treacherous locales.

ISBN 0-933635-82-6

SEA KINGS OF THE PURPLE TOWNS

#2114 **$18.95**

The mercantile center of the Young Kingdoms and a haven for adventurers.

ISBN 1-56882-000-3

CALL OF CTHULHU

A horror roleplaying game set in the world of the Cthulhu Mythos, as described by H. P. Lovecraft, the father of modern horror.

CALL OF CTHULHU

#2336 **$21.95**

Contains everything that you need to play, except dice. Includes character generation, extensive background, notes on the Dreamlands and playing in the 1990s and 1890s.

ISBN 0-933635-86-9

TERROR AUSTRALIS

#2319 **$17.95**

A source book for the Land Down Under.

ISBN 0-933635-40-0

THE GREAT OLD ONES

#2321 **$17.95**

Six different looks at particular Great Old Ones or their influences.

ISBN 0-933635-38-9

MANSIONS OF MADNESS

#2327 **$17.95**

Five frightening adventures.

ISBN 0-933635-63-X

FATAL EXPERIMENTS

#2328 **$18.95**

Three adventures including an encounter with the King in Yellow.

ISBN 0-933635-72-9

BLOOD BROTHERS

#2329 **$18.95**

13 one-night scenarios, all based on familiar themes typical of the kind found in B-movies.

0-933635-69-9

RETURN TO DUNWICH

#2330 **$18.95**

An accursed backwoods town.

ISBN 0-933635-71-0

HORROR ON THE ORIENT EXPRESS

#2331 **$39.95**

Our largest adventure pack ever, set on and along the route of the Orient Express.

ISBN 0-933635-76-1

TALES OF THE MISKATONIC VALLEY

#2334 **$18.95**

Six adventures in settings along the Miskatonic River.

ISBN 0-933635-83-4

FEARFUL PASSAGES

#2335 **$18.95**

A collection of adventures focusing on transportation in the 1920s.

ISBN 0-933635-87-7

ESCAPE FROM INNSMOUTH

#2338 **$20.95**

A complete description of shadowy Innsmouth.

ISBN 0-933635-65-6

THE THING AT THE THRESHOLD

#2339 **$16.95**

A campaign from Arkham to England to the Dead Sea.

ISBN 0-933635-90-7

BLOOD BROTHERS II

#2340 **$18.95**

They're B-movies, they're bad, and they're back.

ISBN 0-933635-91-5

ADVENTURES IN ARKHAM COUNTRY

#2342 **$18.95**

Adventures which take place in or around Arkham, Dunwich, Innsmouth, and Kingsport.

ISBN 1-56882-004-6

INVESTIGATOR'S COMPANION

VOLUME I

#2343 **$10.95**

Are there flashlights in the 1920s? Flashbulbs? Discover the types of equipment, research facilities,

and firearms available
ISBN 1-56882-007-0

KEEPER'S COMPENDIUM

#2344 **$12.95**

A supplement to the CALL OF CTHULHU rules created especially for keepers. Expands upon Forbidden Books, Secret Cults, Alien Races, and Mysterious Places.
ISBN 1-56882-010-0

INVESTIGATOR'S COMPANION

VOLUME II

#2346 **$10.95**

More exciting data on the 1920s, focusing on the Occupations and Skills from that era.
ISBN 1-56882-018-6

YE BOOKE OF MONSTRES

#2349 **$10.95**

A collection of new horrible and generally unfriendly creatures for use with CALL OF CTHULHU.
ISBN 1-56882-019-4

CTHULHU CASEBOOK

#3305 **$19.95**

Nine terrifying adventures.
ISBN 0-933635-67-2

CURSE OF CTHULHU

#3306 **$19.95**

Visit Egypt, Transylvania, the moon, and the alien library at Celaeno.
ISBN 0-933635-74-5

CTHULHU NOW

#3307 **$16.95**

A source book for the 1990s.
ISBN 0-933635-51-6

H.P.L.'s DREAMLANDS

#3308 **$16.95**

The lands beyond the wall of sleep.
ISBN 0-933635-97-4

GASLIGHT ADVENTURES

DARK DESIGNS

#2332 **$18.95**

Explore the occult in 1890s England.
ISBN 0-933635-75-3

SACRAMENTS OF EVIL

#2345 **$18.95**

Six adventures set in 1890s England, the green and pleasant land at the height of its glory.
ISBN 1-56882-015-1

MODERN DAY

AT YOUR DOOR

#2326 **$17.95**

Uncover the secret agenda of the Full Wilderness environmental organization.
ISBN 0-933635-64-8

THE STARS ARE RIGHT!

#2337 **$18.95**

Modern era. A radio telescope detects the presence of an alien body.
ISBN 0-933635-88-5

GUIDES AND SOURCEBOOKS

FIELD GUIDE TO CREATURES OF THE DREAMLANDS

#5107 **$15.95**

27 frightening creatures from beyond the wall of sleep.
ISBN 0-933635-52-4

COC5 KEEPER'S KIT

#5110 **$14.95**

A keeper's screen measuring 40" across, Lovecraft Country adventure, bookmark, condensed rules and tables, special character sheets, and scale model of the Strange High House In The Mist.
ISBN 1-933635-96-6

INVESTIGATOR SHEETS

#5111 **$8.95**

A pad of two-color forms useful to every Cthulhu player.
ISBN 1-56882-002-X

DIRE DOCUMENTS

#5112 **$8.95**

Letter heads, commitment papers, release papers, and other items.
ISBN 1-56882-003-8

PENDRAGON

Based on the legends of King Arthur, Lancelot, Guenever, and the Knights of the Round Table.

PENDRAGON

#2716 **$26.95**

The basic rules; includes everything that you need to play, except dice. New features include Celtic magic system.
ISBN 1-56882-006-2

THE BOY KING

#2708 **$18.95**

A complete campaign covering the entire reign of King Arthur.
ISBN 0-933635-78-8

SAVAGE MOUNTAINS

#2710 **$18.95**

Four adventures set in the wild mountains of legendary Wales.
ISBN 0-933635-81-8

BLOOD & LUST

#2711 **$18.95**

A medium-length campaign set across Britain.
ISBN 0-933635-84-2

PERILOUS FOREST

#2712 **$18.95**

Extensive background for western Cumbria and the Perilous Forest.
ISBN 0-933635-44-3

PAGAN SHORE

#2713 **$18.95**

Extensive background informaion about the mysterious realm of Ireland, her people, and her hisotry. Complete with rules on creating Irish characters and Irish magic.
ISBN 1-56882-016-X

THE SPECTRE KING

#2714 **$18.95**

Six heroic adventures.
ISBN 0-933635-94-X

ELFQUEST

ELFQUEST is a fantasy roleplaying game based on the best-selling graphic novels of the same name, published by Father Tree Press.

SEA ELVES

#2603 **$7.95**

Background and details about a band of isolated elves living on an archipelago.
ISBN 0-933635-24-9

A CHAOSIUM PRODUCTION

THE HASTUR CYCLE

12 Tales Defining His Monstrous Presence

Ambrose Bierce, Richard W. Champbers, Vincent Starrett, Lin Carter, James Blish, Robert E. Howard, Frank Belknap Long, H.P. Lovecraft, Richard Lupoff, Robert M. Price, Carl Edward Wagner.

edited by Robert M. Price

Chaosium Inc.

HI CHAOSIUM,

I just bought your INVESTIGATORS' COMPANION, VOL. 2 roleplaying supplement. Please send me your latest info and put me on your mailing list for future announcements of new games, books, and supplements.

NAME ______________________________

ADDRESS ______________________________

CITY/STATE/ZIP ______________________________

I also have a friend who would like to receive your free announcements:

NAME OF FRIEND ______________________________

HIS/HER ADDRESS ______________________________

CITY/STATE/ZIP ______________________________

Please list the complete name and address of the store in which you bought this book:

NAME OF LOCAL STORE ______________________________

ADDRESS ______________________________

CITY/STATE/ZIP ______________________________

HOW DO YOU LIKE THIS BOOK? ______________________________

HOW COULD WE IMPROVE IT? ______________________________

YOUR AGE: ❑ 1-11, ❑ 12-14, ❑ 15-18, ❑ 19-25, ❑ 26-35, ❑ 36+

YOUR OCCUPATION: ❑ student, ❑ blue collar, ❑ white collar, ❑ professional, ❑ other: ______________________________

WHERE DID YOU HEAR OF THIS GAME: ❑ friend, ❑ game convention, ❑ magazine article, ❑ magazine advertisement, ❑ book, ❑ hobby store, ❑ Chaosium flier or catalog, ❑ cosmic vibrations, ❑ other: ______________

Chaosium Licensees

The following companies produce licensed products based on our games. If you are interested, write to them for a catalog of their products.

CTHULHU MINIATURES

RAFM CO., INC.
20 PARKHILL RD. EAST
CAMBRIDGE, ONT. N1R 1P2 CANADA

PENDRAGON MINIATURES

LANCE & LASER MODELS, INC.
P.O.BOX 14491
COLUMBUS, OH 43214

FOREIGN LANGUAGE EDITIONS

FRENCH — CALL OF CTHULHU, ARKHAM HORROR, FIELD GUIDES

JEUX DESCARTES
1 RUE DU COLONEL PIERRE AVIA
75503 PARIS CEDEX 15, FRANCE

FRENCH — STORMBRINGER

ORIFLAM
132, RUE DE MARLEY
57158 MONTIGNY LES METZ
FRANCE

GERMAN — PENDRAGON

FANTASY PRODUCTIONS
POSTFACH 260 165
4000 DUSSELDORF 1, GERMANY

GERMAN — CALL OF CTHULHU, STORMBRINGER

QUEEN-CARROMS SPIELWAREN GmBH
ANTWERPENER STRASSE 4
53842 TROISDORF-SPICH
GERMANY

ITALIAN — CALL OF CTHULHU

STRATELIBRI SRL.
VIA PAISIELLO NO. 4
20131 MILANO, ITALY

JAPANESE — MANY TITLES

HOBBY JAPAN CO, LTD.
5-26-5 SENDAGAYA
SHIBUYA-KU TOKYO, 151
JAPAN

SPANISH — CALL OF CTHULHU, STORMBRINGER, PENDRAGON

JOC INTERNACIONAL
SANT HIPÒLIT
08030 BARCELONA, SPAIN

RUNEQUEST

THE AVALON HILL GAME CO.
4517 HARFORD RD.
BALTIMORE, MD 21214

Chaosium Inc. Order Form

950-A 56th St. Oakland CA 94608

QUANTITY	ITEM	PRICE	TOTAL

CA residents add appropriate sales tax for your county: ______

Shipping & Handling: **$5.00**

VISA,M/C **TOTAL:** ______

CHARGE # ______________________________

EXP DATE ______________ DAY PHONE# ______________

SIGNATURE ______________________________

❑ **Please DO NOT ship by UPS**

NAME ______________________________

ADDRESS ______________________________

CITY/STATE ______________________________ ZIP ______________

Chaosium Inc.
950-A 56th Street
Oakland, CA 94608-3129

INVESTIGATORS' COMPANION
VOLUME 2: OCCUPATIONS & SKILLS

Place Stamp Here!